Dear Mum and Dad,

  You said Rosie has gone to a Better Place and I think I know where that is now.

  She'll be with the nightingale. I'm going to find them both and bring them back.

  I promise to look both ways when I cross the road. And I promise I'll do my best not to worry.

Love,
Jasper

'An incredibly moving story
of feeling lost and finding
your way again'
Lisa Thompson, author of *The Day I Was Erased*

'A clever, gentle adventure with a
masterful plot that deals with the
difficult subject of grief so poignantly'
Emma Carroll, author of *The Week at World's End*

'Will break your heart and
mend it together again'
Piers Torday, author of *The Last Wild*

'A stunning tale echoing fables
of old that paints a portrait of grief
with the lightest, deftest touch'
Aisha Bushby, author of *A Pocketful of Stars*

'Brave, unforgettable and beautiful'
Lauren St John, author of *Wave Riders*

'[A] beautifully realised story . . .
tender and hopeful' *Bookseller*

90710 000 517 333

The Hunt for the Nightingale

First published in Great Britain in 2022 by Simon & Schuster UK Ltd

1 3 5 7 9 10 8 6 4 2

Simon & Schuster UK Ltd
1st Floor, 222 Gray's Inn Road, London
WC1X 8HB

www.simonandschuster.co.uk
www.simonandschuster.com.au
www.simonandschuster.co.in

Simon & Schuster Australia, Sydney
Simon & Schuster India, New Delhi

A CIP catalogue record for this book is available
from the British Library.

PB 978-1-3985-1089-0
ebook 978-1-3985-1090-6
audio 978-1-3985-1091-3

Typeset in the UK
Printed and bound by CPI Group (UK) Ltd, Croydon, CR0 4YY

The Hunt for the Nightingale

SARAH ANN JUCKES

illustrated by SHARON KING-CHAI

Simon & Schuster

*For Amelia, Edward and
everyone who stops to listen
S.A.J.*

*For Chloe, Zac, and Casey
S.K-C.*

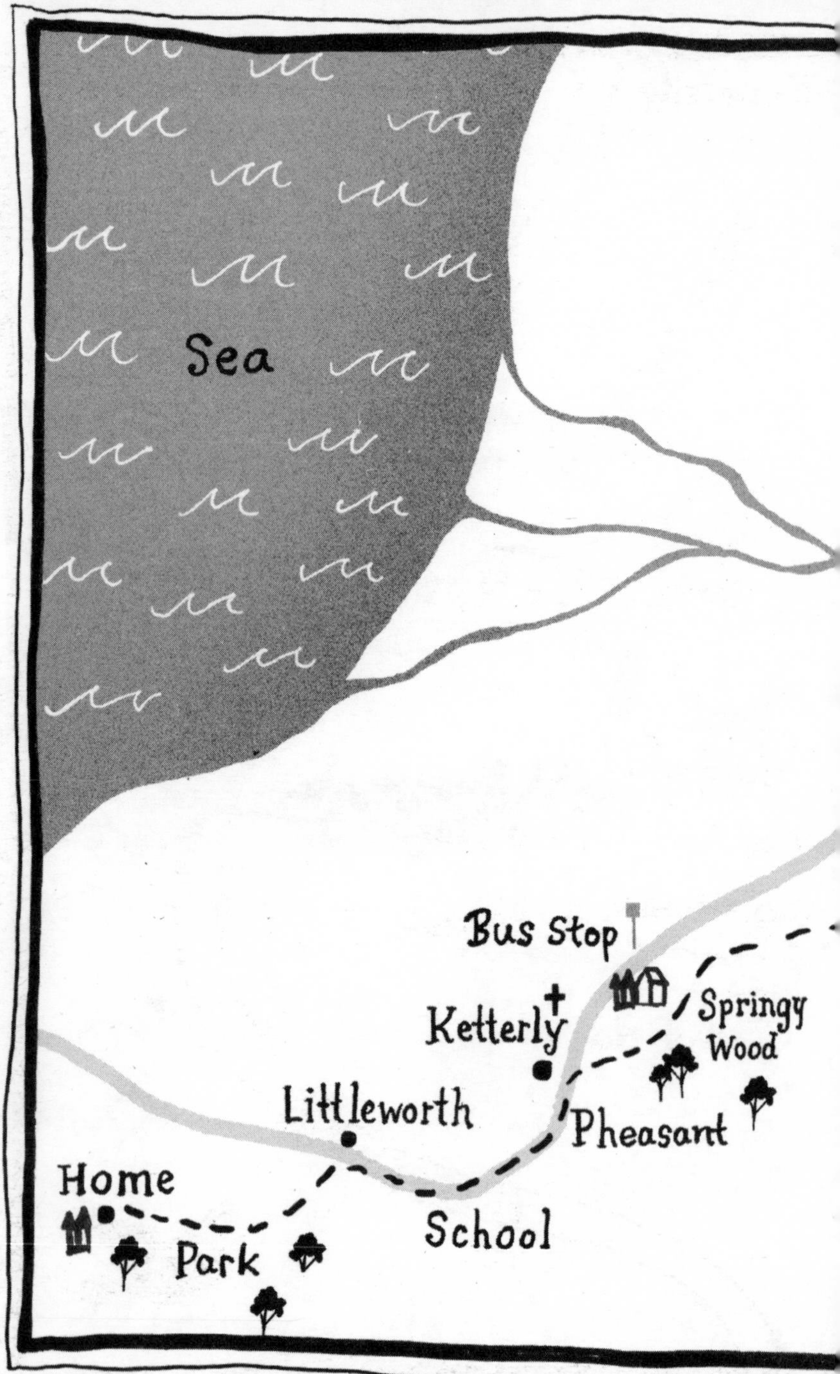
Sea
Bus Stop
Ketterly
Springy Wood
Littleworth
Pheasant
Home
School
Park

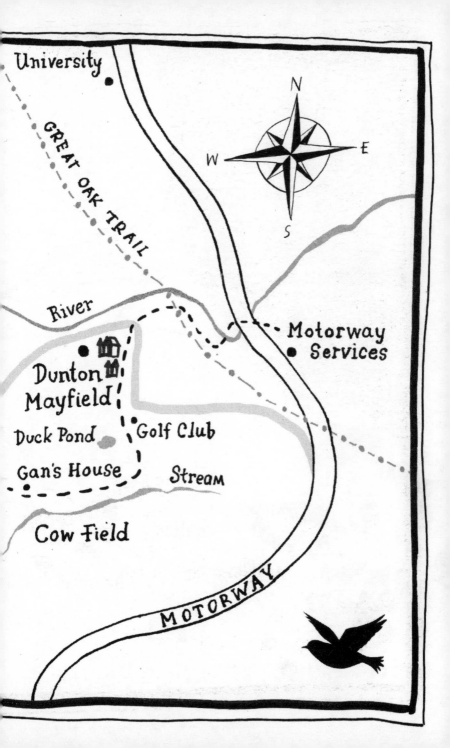

BIRD FACT #1

Nightingales are very difficult to spot

From Rosie and Jasper's Book of Birds

My big sister Rosie says that the first thing you need to do when you're feeling lost, is get your bearings.

At first I thought this might have something to do with bears, but it doesn't. It means you have to work out where you are and try not to panic too much.

Working out where I am right now is easy, because I'm in the tree in the field behind our house. It's tall, but has branches laddering up it so we can climb really high. And there's a flat branch in the middle like a bench hanging in mid-air.

Every spring since always, Rosie and I have sat here together. And we've closed our eyes, held on tight and listened to the nightingale sing in the inky dusk – its *chutter-chatter* splattering against the dark sky like it's a page in an art book.

But the sun is all the way down now. And there's no Rosie next to me. There's no nightingale to listen to.

All I can hear is silence.

BIRD FACT #2

A group of nightingales is called a 'watch'

'Mum? Where's Rosie?'

I call to Mum through the door of the study, and she comes out of the dark, squinting. She looks at me and rubs her eyes. 'Jasper? What are you still doing up? Go to bed, honey – your dad and I are a little busy at the moment.'

I step back, because I know I'm not supposed to

disturb them when they're working and it is past my bedtime. But they've done nothing but lock themselves in their study all week making phone calls and I don't think I can wait any more. 'This is an emergency,' I say. 'And you said I'm allowed to bother you if there's an emergency.'

Mum looks really tired, but she kneels down on the floor and takes my hand. 'Is this the missing bird again? Jasper, we've talked about this. There's nothing your dad and I can do about that. It's a wild bird and compared to everything that's happened, it's really not—'

'I know *you* can't do anything,' I say. 'But Rosie can. She was supposed to come home from university last week and help me find the nightingale. But now they're both missing.'

Mum suddenly goes as pale as a pelican. She drops my hand, but then takes a deep breath and picks it back up again, holding it tighter than before.

'I know this is really hard, Jasper.' She swallows. 'It's hard for your dad and me, too. But Rosie is . . .'

She trails off and I snatch my hand away, looking at my boots and the mud splattered up the sides. I shouldn't be wearing them in the house, but I don't think Mum's noticed. She usually cares a lot about things being neat

4

and clean, but this week, her hair is messy and she smells like she hasn't had a bath for a few days.

Dad comes out of the office and I see his toe poking out of his sock. 'Jasper?' he says. 'What are you doing up?'

Mum stands and whispers to him, but I hear what she says. 'It's the bird again. He wants Rosie to help him find it.'

Dad sighs for a really long time and I lift my head up to see if he's deflated like a balloon. He pinches his eyes under his glasses and then looks at me. 'Your mum and I need a bit of time to sort important things out, buddy. Maybe in a couple of weeks – after the funeral – we can help you find the Night-Tail—'

'Nightingale!' I interrupt.

Dad clenches his jaw and then the phone rings from inside the study and he jumps back inside to answer it.

I look at Mum instead. 'This is important, too.'

She smiles at me, but it's not a proper smile. 'Try not to panic, sweetheart. I know it's hard. Why don't you go read your book – take your mind off things for a while? I know your dad finds it useful to distract himself.'

'But, Mum—'

'Julia!' Dad shouts from inside the study.

5

'I'm coming!' she calls back, before quickly combing her hand through my hair. 'I'll be up soon to say goodnight.'

Dad calls again and Mum sighs and shuts the door behind her.

Nightingale songs are made up of around two hundred different phrases

I don't like losing things. It makes my stomach hurt, and I feel dizzy and sick.

I seem to feel anxious like that more than anyone else in my school. Dad always tells me that I'm worrying over nothing. He always says things like: 'the other children in your class aren't really laughing at you, Jasper,' or that: 'losing your homework isn't the end of the world, you know'.

I'm not sure about that, because Rosie not being here feels like the end of everything, which is probably why I've felt so panicky all this week. But Mum's right – usually I can make the panic go away by thinking about good, true things instead, like everything in our *Book of Birds*.

The *Book of Birds* is a book that Rosie and I have been writing for ages and for ever, and it has everything we know about birds in it. It's the map of my brain, and it's filled with feathers and facts about how to find different types of birds. And when I read it, thoughts about birds take over the worry and I don't feel so bad any more.

There are pages and pages about the nightingale. They say that it's a 'migratory bird', which means it flies away in the summer and comes back to the field behind our house every April. And even though Rosie has flown off to university now because she's nine years older than me, she still promised to drive home every other weekend in April and May, so we could sit in our tree together and listen to the nightingale sing, because it's important.

Two weeks ago, when the nightingale hadn't arrived like it usually does, Rosie sat with me in the dark and the silence.

'I don't like it,' I said. 'The nightingale is usually here by now, isn't it? And now it's May and we've still not heard it once.'

She held my hand in the black. 'You know, I heard there was a nightingale at the M23 motorway services? I bet that's our bird, Jasper. I bet it just got lost on its way home. A bird is only missing until you find it. And I'll find it – I promise.'

And I couldn't really see her face, but Rosie always tells the truth. So I believed her.

'I'll help you,' I said.

And she squeezed my hand, tight. 'We'll do it together, me and you. I'll come back again next weekend.'

That's what she said. She even wrote it herself in our *Book of Birds*.

Rosie and Jasper's hunt for the nightingale

NEXT WEEKEND

She was supposed to come back last Friday – a whole week ago now. I kept looking at our drive after school, waiting for Rosie's rusty purple car to chug up the kerb, with its feathery seat covers and the sunshine music she always plays at full volume. But it was hard to keep a lookout, as Mum and Dad suddenly went out for a long time and left me with our granny, who lives across the road. Granny let me watch cartoons all weekend, but didn't answer any of my questions about where Mum, Dad or Rosie were and kept leaving me to go and sit in her bedroom for some reason.

Mum and Dad were gone so long that I thought maybe they'd got lost, too. And maybe they had, because when they finally came home, they looked as though they didn't know where they were. And Rosie wasn't with them.

I didn't like their expressions. They looked scared and it made me panic. They wanted to hug me and talk to me, but I couldn't listen because my stomach was hurting badly. When I feel anxious like that, the only thing that ever makes me feel like I'm not floating away on an angry, black sea – is birds.

So, while Dad cried, I thought about how nightingales fly three thousand miles to Africa every year.

And while Mum rubbed my hands between hers tightly, I thought about how common nightingales can also be found across Europe and Asia.

I felt bad about not listening properly, but I couldn't help it. I'm supposed to distract myself with nice thoughts when I feel panicky. But the only thing that was left in my head at the end was one thing Dad said:

'Rosie has gone to a Better Place.'

It should have been a nice thing to hear, but it was confusing. What place could possibly be better than sitting in our tree, listening to our nightingale? I am her Better Place.

So where is she?

I turn on my phone and dial her number again, listening to the crackle silence on the other end until her answering machine starts. And I do that again and again, until Mum comes in to say goodnight. But maybe I'm still mad at her for talking about the nightingale like it isn't important, because I pretend to be asleep.

She sits on my bed and watches me for ages. At some point, I do such a good job of pretending that I actually do fall asleep. But when I wake up the next morning, she's gone.

I jump out of bed and run outside still in my pyjamas to check the tree again. And when I can't find Rosie in the branches, I come back to search all the rooms in the house for the millionth time. But all I find is our cat, Fish, asleep on the bathmat.

I go downstairs and jump on the sofa in the living room, so I can pull back the curtains and look on the drive for Rosie's purple car again. But all I can see is the tangled-up front garden and an empty space on the drive next to Mum and Dad's car.

Dad comes in and he's wearing his jumper inside out. He sees me looking out the window and looks sad. 'Maybe we should get you back to school . . .'

I didn't go to school all last week. Mum said I didn't need to go if I didn't want to, and I never want to, so I didn't. It did get boring though – especially because I kept being sent to Granny's. And at her house, there was nothing to distract me from the stomach-ache feeling that something was very wrong.

'It's Saturday,' I say, sliding down the sofa.

Dad looks at his watch, surprised, and then comes to sit with me on the sofa, squeezing my shoulders really tight.

'You know your mum and I love you very much.'

I nod, because I do know that. But him saying it like that makes my heart feel fluttery for some reason, so I wiggle out of his grip and try to escape before he sees that I'm panicking again.

'Where are you going?' he calls as I get to the door.

I stop, but I don't look at him. 'I need to find out where the "Better Place" is,' I mumble.

Dad makes a strange noise in his throat. 'Probably with your silly birds, isn't it,' he says, bitterly.

I am about to argue that birds are magnificent and not silly, but then it clicks.

'Dad, you're a genius!' I leave him in the living room and run up the stairs to my bedroom, where I left our *Book of Birds*. I grab it from the bed and spin through the pages until I find it again.

Rosie and Jasper's hunt for the nightingale

NEXT WEEKEND

Dad's right. If Rosie isn't here with me, then her Better Place must be with the nightingale. And if the nightingale is at the motorway services like she said, now I know where to find her.

She told me last weekend that something is only missing until you find it. So if I can find them both, maybe everything will go back to normal.

Nightingales build cup-shaped nests close to the ground

Before Rosie got her car and left for university, we'd wait ages for Dad to remember to give us lifts to see important things like birds. But Dad isn't usually very good at remembering things that aren't to do with work, so Rosie and I got good at doing things on our own.

I can't drive to the motorway services, because I'm nine. And even if I wanted to ask Mum and Dad for a lift, they've shut the door to their study again which means I'm not allowed in. But there are lots of different ways to get around instead of using a car.

The first thing I need is a map. Rosie has some Ordnance Survey maps in her room, so I take the right one down from her bookshelf. I find the motorway services on one page, and our house on a whole other page, and know that all I need to do is follow the coloured lines from one page to the other.

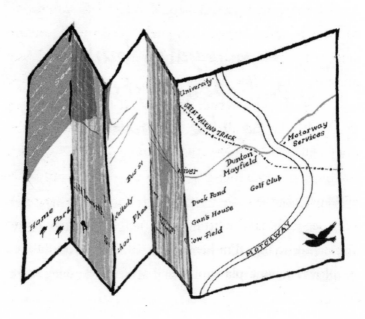

Maps can look confusing at first. All the lines squiggle into each other and there are symbols like a secret spy code. But there's also a square grid drawn over the top and Rosie taught me that reading it is easier if you just take it one tiny square at a time, and use the 'Key' to find out which colour line means what.

I can see a big blue line, snaking across the map. The Key says that's the motorway that links up Rosie's university to our house, but you can't get on that unless you have a car. There are smaller yellow and white roads that I can probably walk on though, because they usually have pavements. One links my house up with my local town called Littleworth. Another line carries on to a town called Dunton Mayfield. And then there are smaller lines like scraggly black-and-red hair that Rosie and I used to follow on our walks, which are footpaths.

I look on the internet and find that there's one bus that will take me almost the whole way there, to the town called Dunton Mayfield in under an hour – and it's leaving soon. And then it's just a walk along a trail and a cycle path to the motorway services, and it's almost like I can see Rosie in the little bit marked 'trees', waving up at me and saying, 'I'm here, Jasper! Come find me!'

Now I have a plan to find Rosie, the stomach-ache

panic I've been feeling all this week feels like it's beginning to fade away.

I go downstairs and fetch the pot of money that Mum and Dad use to go food shopping, and take ten pounds. I feel bad about taking money, because only last year, Mum and Dad said money was tight and we might have to sell our house, which is why they work all the time now making seedy-nut cereal bars for adventurers – so that we have enough to stay here. But maybe if I use it for food and buy chips with it for Rosie and me when I get there, then that will make it okay.

Next, I take my school books and my pencil case out of my backpack and I fill it up with everything I think I'm going to need. And, because I'm prepared, I make a list:

Jasper's list of wilderness survival tools

The Book of Birds
A map
A compass
My binoculars
Food (Lots of seedy-nut bars. A banana.
A chocolate biscuit bar.)

Water
A micro-fibre towel because Dad says you
always need a towel.
Money
My phone
Clean socks
A wind-up torch
A whistle for emergencies
My walking boots, which are the shoes
that are okay to get muddy.
A coat, even though it's quite sunny.
Suncream
A sun hat

If I was going to go overnight, then I would take a camping stove and a sleeping bag and things like that, but the bus is in thirty minutes from the station down the road and I'll probably be there just after lunch, so I think I'll be okay.

I eat some toast and make sure Fish the cat has enough food and water, and her litter tray is clean. I find her asleep on Rosie's pillow and give her a lot of chin-scratches goodbye. And then I stand outside Mum and Dad's study for a long time, wondering if I should knock. But inside I can hear typing and sighing and coffee cups being picked up and put down, and all of that usually means I shouldn't disturb them.

So I write a note instead, and leave it for them on the kitchen counter.

Dear Mum and Dad,
You said Rosie has gone to a Better Place and I think I know where that is now. She'll be with the nightingale. I'm going to find them both and bring them back.
I promise to look both ways when I cross the road. And I promise I'll do my best not to worry.
Love, Jasper

The body of a swallow is not much bigger than a matchbox

My house is at the very end of Littleworth town, before the houses turn into meadows and sheep fields and woods.

I walk past the local shop, where Dad goes to buy his newspaper most days and I can sometimes buy sweets or a wildlife magazine, depending on which one I want most. Usually it's the magazine. And I walk past the play park where I saw a sparrowhawk once.

The bus depot is a building in the middle of a circle of road like a roundabout. The timetable on the internet said there was only one bus that would go to Dunton Mayfield today, and it would be at stop four. I'd hoped that it might be a double-decker bus, which would mean I could sit at the top at the front and watch the whole world spin below me like I was flying. But this one is just a single-decker and looks a bit dirty.

I stand back nervously and watch everyone get on. I recognize a girl called Lulu who's on her own, like I am. She's a few years older than me, so she's at secondary school now, but I remember her big glasses and long braids from when she was in Year Six. I also remember that she used to be the star of all our school concerts, because she could dance like a bird of paradise.

I shift about a bit and try to 'act confident', like Dad is always telling me to do. I put my shoulders back and chin in the air and hope that Lulu can't see how sweaty my hands are. Her glasses magnify her eyes a lot and it feels like they're magnifying me as she looks in my direction. At school, it sometimes feels like the others in my class look and laugh at me, so I've got used to trying to hide. My teacher, Ms Li, says that isn't true, but Lulu peering at me still makes me feel nervous.

I'm worried that she might come over and start speaking to me, but she carefully steps onto the bus and I breathe a sigh of relief. It's me next and the bus driver is looking at me like he's wondering what's taking me so long to climb aboard.

I grip the ten-pound note and it's slippery from where I've been holding it. The bus driver has stern eyes and white eyebrows, and a long nose like a beak, that makes him look sort of like an American bald eagle. But instead of that making me feel better, it makes me feel like he might peck off my fingers.

The panic in my chest flaps up my throat and I shout: 'One return to Dunton Mayfield, please.'

DUNTON MAYFIELD

The bus driver looks me up and down, so I grip the *Book of Birds* and try to think about facts I know about bald eagles.

AMERICAN BALD EAGLES

Bald eagles are big and fast, with long legs and talons, which means they can catch their prey in mid-air if they need to. That's quite a good skill to have, because one of their favourite foods is other birds.

Usually bird facts make me feel better, but that one just made the driver look even meaner. I throw the money at him instead and he slowly gives me a ticket and six pound coins in change. He starts up his engine, so I run quickly to the closest seat there is, away from Lulu sitting at the back.

The bus starts to back up with the doors still open. And I know I could run right back through them, back home and into bed, where there aren't any loud engines, grumpy bus drivers, or people who might recognize me from school.

But Rosie is missing. And when you lose something you love, you do everything you can to find it.

I grip the sides of the seat and feel a bit sick as the bus pulls out and starts rumbling over bumps in the road. We go past my school, and it feels strange seeing the gates closed after not being there for a whole week. The toast I had for breakfast churns around my stomach like it might jump back up out of my mouth at any moment.

I'm used to being the one who worries about things like bus journeys, but the last time Rosie and I were on a bus together, she was the nervous one. We were going to visit her university for the first time, before she officially got accepted. She wasn't sure if the course was the right one for her, or if she'd feel at home in a whole different place.

Mum and Dad were too busy trying to make us enough money to keep our house to come with us, so to make her feel better, Rosie and I sat together on the top deck, trying to spot birds. We saw a whole flight of swallows, which you can spot because of their forked tails. They were flying a loop-the-loop over the fields, looking for insects to eat, and it made our worry disappear.

When we got to the university, we met a student who was wearing a hat with a picture of an otter on and the words 'This is my otter hat', which we both thought was hilarious. He said his name was David and took us for a tour of the 'campus', which is the name for where the classrooms and houses camp out together. On it were trees and a big lake with ducks and even a heron. And then we went into a building where the lessons that they called lectures took place, and it was much bigger and posher than my classroom at school. Everyone sits in lines behind long desks that are on stairs that go up and up like a theatre.

We sat at one of the benches as a teacher told everyone about the lessons on the course, and some of them sounded boring, but some of them were about birds. And Rosie put her hand up and asked all these questions, but no one was sighing at her and asking her to be quiet, like Dad sometimes did. They didn't even seem to mind that she'd brought me along, when there were no other children there. Everyone listened and nodded and I suddenly got sad, because I could tell that Rosie would love it there, and that meant she would be going away.

After the talk, I went outside to sit on the grass and she sat down next to me.

'What's wrong, Jasper?'

'You're going to leave me alone, aren't you?'

She took my hand and held it tightly. 'You're not alone, silly. Mum and Dad—'

But she stopped and didn't say anything, because we both knew that they're busy all the time and don't really count as there at all.

Instead, Rosie got a felt-tip pen out of her pocket and started drawing on my hand with it. I tried to see what it was, but she wouldn't let me see until it was done. It was a bit wonky, because Rosie is good at wildlife facts and being a sister, but she is bad at drawing. But I could tell from the tail that it was a swallow and it looked like this:

Swallow

'Swallows fly thousands and thousands of miles away every single year, but they always fly back again. And even when I'm not around, you'll never be alone, Jasper.'

I traced my finger around the outside of the drawing. 'How often will you come back?'

'Whenever you need me to.'

Her face looked like she was telling the truth, because that's what she did, always. And I hugged her, because Rosie was happy, and even though I knew I'd miss her, I was happy for her, too.

The bus jumps and an old lady who is standing up looks worried about holding on, so I get up so she can sit down. I shuffle under the arms of people to where I can see out of the front window better. We're hurtling down a long country road now with trees either side. Some of them have cut-out square branches at the top, from where the double-decker buses have gone by, and it looks like a puzzle that has pieces missing.

I look at the place on my hand where Rosie drew the swallow, but it rubbed off a whole year ago. Remembering the drawing always used to calm me down, but seeing it gone now reminds me that Rosie is gone too. Even though she promised to come back.

I always thought that things were just facts, like that birds would always migrate back home in the spring and Rosie would always come home when she said she would. But maybe some facts can change.

My stomach twists horribly, so I quickly look at my watch. I still have forty minutes of standing left and then a walk before I can find Rosie and set the facts right again. I'm half-wondering if I can ask the bus driver to hurry up, when something out the front window catches my eye. A flash of bright blue and red feathers. And suddenly, there's a pheasant in the road and the bus isn't slowing down. And I shout and someone else presses the bell, but the pheasant doesn't see the bus and I don't think the bus sees the pheasant and—

THUMP.

Baby pheasant chicks can fly when they're just twelve days old

'You hit it!' I shout, pushing past people to the very front, where the driver's white eyebrows are knitted together.

'Back behind the line!' he shouts and I take a step back, because that is the rule.

'You hit the pheasant!' I say from behind him. 'You have to see if it's okay.'

The driver looks at me. 'Calm down,' he says. 'It was only a bird.'

Only a bird! The driver just hit something living and real and beautiful and he won't even go back to check it's okay.

I ring and ring and ring the bell and the passengers start groaning. Someone is telling me off from the back of the bus, but I don't care, because I need to see if the pheasant is okay.

The bus slows down and the doors open at a stop in the middle of nowhere. I run off the bus and the driver shouts something at me, but there's no time to listen. I go back down the road a bit, making sure to stick to the pavement. I look for feathers on the tarmac or traces of blood and all that worry feels like cold in my bones.

The pavement runs out, becoming a grass verge at the side of the road instead. I stop, looking left and right. But I can't see anything.

'Any sign of it?'

I spin round and see that Lulu has followed me off the bus. I feel myself getting hot and look down at my boots, shaking my head.

We both stand with our hands on our hips and look out into the bush beside the pavement.

'Maybe he flew off?' she says.

I chew on my lip. 'Maybe.' I want to tell her that pheasants can't always fly very far, because it takes a lot of energy for them to take off, but I feel nervous with her peering at me.

'Let's look in the bush on the other side, then.'

We look both ways and cross the road. Lulu looks over the top of the bush to the other side because she's taller than I am, but we don't see the pheasant.

'Sorry, Jasper,' she says. 'But if he's not here, then that probably means he's okay.'

I flick my head up. 'You know my name?'

'Of course,' she says. 'You go to the same primary school I went to, don't you? You made all those bird-fact posters in the hall – I always liked how big and neat your handwriting was.'

I blink at her. Ms Li and I made those fact posters together when I was feeling anxious at lunchtime. It can happen sometimes at school, because I can get nervous about talking to other kids, even though they let me play football with them whenever I want. It felt good to have my pictures on the wall, big and bold for everyone to

33

see, but I never thought about anyone reading the facts. Especially someone as popular as Lulu.

She smiles at me. 'I thought it was you when you ran off the bus. I wanted to make sure you were okay, and not lost like your pheasant and Buster.'

I bite my lip. 'Who's Buster?'

She pulls open the bag on her shoulder and shows me a wad of paper the size of the stack Dad has on his desk at home. 'Buster is my dog. He's always running off.'

She hands me one of the pieces of paper.

MISSING DOG

Answers to 'Buster'.

Buster is a greyhound who loves chasing after rabbits.

He was last seen in Ketterly on Friday 14th May and hasn't come back home.

Please keep a lookout for him and let Lulu know if you see him on

01345 765 654

'He ran off yesterday,' she says. 'I'm going to put these posters up where I lost him, in the fields over there. Do you want to help?'

'Sorry,' I say, 'but I should probably get back on the bus.'

'That's okay,' she says. We both turn round, hunting for the bus at the bus stop back up the road.

'Oh!' she says, as something sinks inside of me like a stone in a pond.

The road is empty.

The bus has left without me.

BIRD FACT #7

Some owls can turn their heads more than 270 degrees

Rosie always says that the reason people get lost is because they're either not paying attention, or they're panicking.

I don't know where I am, because I was too busy

worrying about the pheasant and not paying attention, and I think that means I'm lost. And being lost means that it's going to take me even longer to find Rosie.

But that doesn't mean I need to panic.

Lulu looks concerned. Usually, someone staring at me like this makes me feel self-conscious, but her glasses sort of make her look like she has owl-eyes. It's helping to calm me down, in the same way reading facts about owls in the *Book of Birds* does.

I take out my map and I lay it down on the grass by the side of the road to get my bearings.

'Do you know where we are?' I ask her.

She looks down at the map, but then shakes her head. 'Sorry, I can't see that. I'm partially sighted. My glasses help me see bigger shapes, but small things like maps are too patchy to read.'

'Oh,' I say. 'I don't have a bigger version, but maybe I can read the map for you. Do you know any landmarks close by?'

'This is Ketterly, like it says on the missing poster my dad made.' She gets one out of her bag again and gives it to me, so I can see how it's spelt. 'My grandma lives down that road.' She points ahead past the bus stop we got off at, to a little road that turns left. 'Down there is

37

a church and the town hall I have my dance classes in, if that's helpful.'

It's really helpful. I find my house again, and the bus station, and then I follow the orange road up and over the page to the other side, where I see the words 'Ketterly' on the edge. There's a little cross sign for church and town hall.

I let out my breath. 'I'm not lost. I know exactly where I am.'

I'm feeling quite proud of myself for working all that out, when I realize that I'm only just on the side of the page. The bus was supposed to drop me off at Dunton Mayfield, which is squares and squares away, and I don't think there are any other buses coming today.

'If you like, you can help me find Buster and then come to my grandma's house for tea. She makes the best cakes,' Lulu says. 'I'm here every weekend for dance lessons, so I know the way on my own now. Did you want to come?'

'No!' I accidentally snap. 'I have to find my sister and I'm going to be late.'

I fold the map up and put it in my bag and when I stand up, Lulu is still staring at me.

I suddenly realize why she's asking for help. How

are you supposed to find something when you can't see very well?

I look at my watch. 'I suppose I can help you until one o'clock. But then I really need to go, because I don't know how long it will take to get there, now.'

She smiles wide. 'Great. It's always nicer to look for things with company, isn't it? Come on – I'll show you the field he got lost in.'

We walk until we come to a gate that leads into a field. I check the map and see that it's marked with a red dotted line, which means it's okay to walk through there.

The ground is muddy and squelches under my walking boots, and I'm pleased I was prepared and brought them instead of my school trainers, or else Mum would hit the roof.

The field is big and square and has long grass in the middle of it, with a path around the outside. 'Which way?' I say.

Lulu points right. 'I was walking there with my grandma when I let him off the lead yesterday. Then he saw a rabbit and just ran off into the grass – he's really fast.' She grips her sides like she remembers running after him and getting stitch, which I get all the time at football practice.

'Okay,' I say. 'Let's look there, first. Maybe he came back, looking for you, too.'

We walk around the field towards a huge tree that looks like the sycamore we climb in the field behind our home. Lulu walks slower than I do, being careful where to put her feet, but her footsteps are so quiet that it sounds like I'm walking alone.

'You'd be really good at finding birds,' I say shyly. 'You have the perfect quiet walk.'

She smiles. 'Maybe it's the dancing. It definitely helps me to be more sure-footed, which is useful when you sometimes can't see the ground properly.'

The earth is ridged with tractor tracks and cracked like dry elephant skin, so it's difficult to walk on. 'Is Buster your seeing-eye dog?'

She laughs. 'No – seeing-eye dogs are much better trained. My dad found Buster when he ran away from a rescue centre and I fell in love with him. He'd make a rubbish seeing-eye dog, but he's a wonderful friend. And having him around makes me feel calm, even when there's not much light and I can't see well, you know?'

I nod, because I do know. 'That's how I feel about birds and my sister Rosie.' My heart is fluttering again, speaking to Lulu. But it's not the normal panic-flutter; it feels different. It feels nice, actually.

We get to the tree and slow down. 'Then you know exactly,' she says.

I smile and look around, pretending that I'm a barn owl with super eyesight that can see a tiny mouse from far away.

I can't see a mouse or a dog, but I tell Lulu about the time Rosie and I saw a barn owl in real life.

Owls are nocturnal, which means they like to be awake during the night and find their food in the dark. They have big eyes that have adapted to seeing in dim light, but they also have amazing hearing. Their ears are wonky on their heads, so one is higher than the other one, and this helps them work out exactly where their prey is. It's like they can draw a map in their minds just from sounds.

In order to find a barn owl, Rosie and I had to think like a barn owl, too. Because they only come out at night, we made a plan to tiptoe out of the house at dusk, but Dad was in the kitchen and saw Rosie before she could reach the door.

'Rosie?' he said, wiping his hands down his apron. 'Come over here and try this. We're thinking of introducing a new flavour to the nut bars. I could do with my sous chef's opinion – too much caramel?'

Rosie rolled her eyes. Her and Dad used to make seedy-nut bars all the time when I was too young to go out on adventures with her, but for ages, her and Dad seem to have been living on whole separate planets.

She pushed me out of the door, so Dad wouldn't see that she was sneaking me out, too. 'Sounds good, Dad. Got to go see an owl though, so maybe later?'

I could see Dad's face through the crack of the door and he looked sad. I wanted to tell Rosie that finding an owl could wait until the next day, and that maybe we could all make a new recipe tonight instead, because it smelt delicious. But then Dad got mad.

'Fine – go and see your owl then. It's clearly more important.'

Rosie sighed. 'Dad – owls *are* important. They're important to me and—'

But Dad had turned away and was waving his hand and not listening any more, so Rosie stomped into her shoes and dragged me off into the dark, muttering about how Dad doesn't listen to anything she ever says.

'But you didn't listen to his seedy-nut bar recipe either?' I said.

Rosie glared at me and I think she was going to say something else when we heard it. The barn owl – screeching like a ghost from the shadows.

We walked into the fields towards the sound. It was so dark that I couldn't see the ground or anything around me, just the faint glow of the moon behind the clouds and some stars peeking through. But I could hear the dry leaves and sticks under our shoes rustling and snapping, like we were walking on bubble-wrap. I could also hear Rosie's still-angry breaths and behind that, a fox screaming somewhere, as well as the roaring sound of distant roads. But there in the fields, it was all breath and sticks and owls.

Then Rosie stopped so suddenly that I jumped. She put her hand out and dragged me in front of her and I could feel her tickly whispers in my ear.

'There. On the fence post. Listen.'

I listened. And it was silent until suddenly the barn owl hissed again and I saw it. Balanced on a fence post up ahead, watching us.

Its white feathers almost looked glow-in-the-dark in the shadows, and its heart-shaped face seemed surprised to see us.

'Shhh!' Rosie said in my ear, even though I wasn't making any noise.

We watched it watch us and my throat felt clogged with silence. It was a real-life barn owl and we had found it, just by listening.

'Hey!' I say to Lulu. 'That's it.'

I take my bag off my shoulder and rummage around for the whistle I packed.

'What are you doing?' she asks.

'You don't need to be able to see well to be able to find something,' I say. 'You can use sound, too. Sound, like a dog whistle.'

I put the whistle between my lips, and I blow hard. It makes a long, high noise like when someone pops a balloon near your ears and you hear a ringing in them for a bit. But this ringing goes out across the field and stops the birds in the tree right in the middle of their song.

'Oh!' Lulu says, blinking around the field.

I can't see a dog anywhere, so I blow it again. And I'm thinking about packing it back away, when she clutches my arm.

'I think I hear him! Blow it again!'

I do, and the grass in the field rustles like scrunched-up paper as something big comes running through it. It scurries out the other side and spins round, and it's a skinny brown dog that looks an awful lot like—

'Buster!' Lulu shouts.

Buster comes whipping right up to her and jumps up at her legs so hard that she falls over and gets mud up her back, but she doesn't care because she has found her dog and they hold each other tight and—

I run away.

Pigeon

BIRD FACT #8

Pigeons are thought to be one of the most intelligent birds on earth

I'm breathing so fast that I can see spots.

I put my hands on my knees and hear Lulu shouting my name behind me, so I crouch down low and hide behind the long grass. It was nice seeing that Buster was okay and how happy Lulu was to find him, but then that just reminded me that I'm still so far away from finding Rosie at the motorway services, and I miss her like a tree with a hole in its branches. I don't do a very good job of hiding though, because Lulu soon finds me and Buster jumps into my lap to lick my face.

'You ran away before I could thank you!' she says, sitting down in the dusty dirt with me and pulling Buster back. 'He was in this field all along. That was really clever – I'm definitely going to get a whistle now. It's funny, isn't it, how some things can be lost, but not that far away at all?'

She's looking at me in that magnified way again and I rub my face. 'My sister is with the nightingale and it's quite far away.'

She reaches out to pat my shoe. 'You'll get there though. You're probably one of the cleverest people I've met, so I know you will.'

I look up at her. 'I am?'

She smiles. 'Of course! You know all these facts about birds and how to call dogs and stuff. If anyone can find anything, it's you.'

I feel a huge wave of warmth all the way to my toes and I'm suddenly really pleased I met Lulu at the bus stop – even though I thought it would be a disaster.

She stands up, dusting herself off. 'You can still come back to my grandma's for some cake? I can go with you on your walk after then, if you like.'

I shake my head. 'Thank you, but I really should get going . . .'

She shrugs and pulls Buster close. 'All right then. Keep up that cleverness, Jasper. And next time, don't be afraid to say hello, okay?'

I wave her and Buster off, and feel a bit sad watching them go. I'm half-thinking of running after them and asking them if I can join them for cake after all, when I hear a flapping noise. I look up as a wood pigeon lands near my feet.

FACTS ABOUT PIGEONS

Scientists at Oxford University did a study on how pigeons find their way home. They found that pigeons use landmarks as signposts and even follow roads like they're in cars.

I tear my eyes away from Lulu and Buster growing smaller in the distance and I lay my map out again. I could follow the road the bus was going down to find Rosie, like a pigeon would. It goes all the way to Dunton Mayfield, where I need to get to. Some roads don't have pavements though, so I dig my phone out of my pocket to check. I forgot to charge it when I made those calls last night and the battery is low, so I need to be quick.

I go to 'Maps' and 'Satellite view', which is where you can see the whole world from above as a picture, rather than squiggly lines. It's clever enough to know right where I am in the field, and shows me as a blue dot on the map.

I follow the road on the screen for a bit and see that not far away, the pavement disappears again, like I thought it might.

I scrunch my face up, because I promised Mum and Dad in my note that I would look both ways before crossing a road, but that's hard to do when you're walking along one. And it's not like I have wings and can fly above them like a pigeon.

I put my phone back in my bag and look at the paper map for a better route with red footpath lines. The lines criss-cross the road and go around farms and houses, but they end up right where I need to go.

The Key in the corner says every two centimetres on the map is one kilometre in real life. Rosie taught me that every square drawn over the map is two centimetres by two centimetres, which means that it's one kilometre by one kilometre.

It's fifteen squares to get to the bit where it says Dunton Mayfield on the map, and some of that is a bit windy up and down, so it might even be a bit further. I'm not sure what was the furthest Rosie and I ever went through the fields behind our house, but I think this might be further than I've ever walked before in my whole life.

I just need to be prepared.

It's important to make sure you're eating the right food, drinking lots of water and wearing the right clothing when you go for long walks. I know I have the right food, because I have a lot of seedy-nut bars and Mum and Dad make those especially for people going on adventures. There's even a photo of a person cycling on the front of the bar with the raisins in, and someone else standing on the top of a mountain on the one with the coconut in.

It's one o'clock now, so I eat a seedy-nut bar and the banana, and drink some water, and throw a bit of each to the pigeon, too.

At the moment, the weather is nice. It's not cold, even though the sun is behind some grey clouds in the sky, so I don't need my coat. I put some suncream on my face though, because once Dad got sunburnt on his nose on a day like this and he looked like a clown.

Once I'm kitted up and feeling prepared, I put the compass and binoculars around my neck and fold the map up so I can just carry it in one hand. I stare at the path in front of me, leading me right to where I know Rosie must be. For a moment, I get a flash of panic like electricity in my bones, and it makes me want to run back to Lulu again, even though I can't see her at all now.

But then I remember what Lulu said about me being clever enough to find anything. And I don't know – maybe I am. Maybe if I just did brave things like say hello to a kind girl, I can accomplish anything.

Even find a missing sister.

I take a deep breath and start walking.

BIRD FACT #9

Songbirds take lots of mini-breaths every second so they can keep singing

The first square on the map links to a black-dash line through a green patch with tree symbols, which the map says is called 'Springy Wood'. The Key says that a black-dash line means a 'path', and when I get to it, there's a wooden sign pointing to some trees, just like the map said.

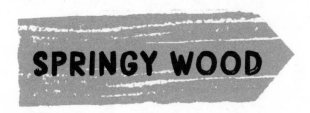

SPRINGY WOOD

The path here is much nicer than the one around the field. It's still muddy, but wide, with dog poo bins on the edges. The trees are planted far apart at first, but then they start coming together more as I walk, and cross their branches at the top, so I feel like I'm in the middle of a football strategy huddle.

It's darker in here, but I don't mind because all around me are birds and birds and birds. I can't see any, but I can hear them, and all together they sound like a whole orchestra. I keep walking, but my ears are trying to pick the songs out from each other. I can hear a wren, because they're small but loud, and almost sound like a machine gun. And when that stops, I can hear a chaffinch replying with little bursts of notes that's like being rained on in fat drops. And I think I can also hear a goldfinch, but they're a bit twittery and quite hard to pick out.

I pick up my binoculars and zoom into the trees. I catch the wings of a blackbird and a yellow flash of a great tit. It's always exciting to hear a bird and then go hunting through the trees to try and catch a glimpse of it. Kind of like collecting, although I can't take any of them home. I do always put pictures and stories about them in our *Book of Birds* when I get back though.

It was Rosie's idea that we start writing that. We use it to keep track of the birds we find and that we still need to catch a glimpse of, in this country and in others all around the world. When I look through it later, I can remember how exciting it was when we spotted them, or think of the ones I wish I could find in the wild.

This story is definitely going to get stuck in beside the others when I get home.

I come out of Springy Wood into an alleyway around the back of some people's houses. Their gardens are neat and tidy, not like ours at home. Mum used to do a lot of gardening when I was small and she was still an accountant. She used to take Rosie and me to the garden centre, where we could pick out garden gnomes and play in the sheds. But there's not enough time to do that sort of thing any more.

A few of these houses have bird feeders hanging up in their gardens, which is a good way to see birds from your window, as well as helping them in the winter. I see an old lady putting out washing on a line next to one, as a sparrow swoops in and steals some seeds from it. She looks up at me and I think of Lulu and give her a big smile and she smiles back, even though I realize after that she was holding a pair of pants, which might have been embarrassing.

I look both ways and wait for a car to go by before I cross the road out of the alleyway, and then I look until I find a stile with a wonky post and a yellow arrow, which my compass says is pointing north-west – just where I want to go.

Rosie once said that you could walk around the whole country following footpath arrows if you wanted to, which I always thought sounded exciting. Whenever she drives me around in her purple car with the feather seats, I keep my eye out for the arrows from the car window and wonder where they're pointing to. And now I know they were all pointing right towards her.

I hop up onto the first wooden step and throw my

leg over, and I'm feeling like a brave explorer, until I realize that I've just wandered into a cow field.

I stop dead, rooted to the spot.

There are probably about twenty black-and-white cows in front of me. Some are sitting down, but some are standing up and looking at me. They're big, and make me feel small, and I remember the one time Dad ever took me for a walk after he started his business with Mum, when a bull nearly killed us both.

It was last summer, and Dad had suddenly decided that I should go fishing with him, like his dad used to do when he was my age. Some of the others in my class go fishing, and so I knew that most people go to a special fishing shop to get maggots to use as bait. But Dad said that was cheating and that we'd be getting our bait from the place he'd got it from when he was my age – from a cow pat.

Rosie thought the idea of me sticking my hands in a load of cow poo to find worms was hilarious, so she came along too.

We set off early in the morning, so the sun was still

smashed and smeared red in the sky. Rosie and I were used to walking, so we were in front and talking about the birds in the morning chorus, whilst Dad huffed and puffed behind us. The chorus sounded like a wall of noise and it was difficult to break through it to pick out the different birds, but altogether it was beautiful. That was until Dad started grumbling at Rosie for turning our trip about fish into one about birds. Rosie immediately snapped back, like she always does, and it was annoying, because all that arguing was drowning out the birdsong.

We got to the cow field eventually. There was only one cow in there and it was waking up. Rosie stopped shouting and held Dad's sleeve.

'That's a bull, Dad.'

He put his head up, but I could tell that he was still miffed, because he shrugged her off him. 'It's fine.'

'But, Dad—'

'You don't know everything, Rosie,' he snapped, making the bull look over at us from the middle of the field. 'I've been doing this all my life.'

He hopped over the fence, even though there was no stile or yellow arrow saying it was okay, and pulled me over. I was looking at the bull, who looked big and mean. Dad had his lips pinched tightly though, which usually meant I wasn't to say anything.

He walked me to a big cow pat and crouched down, putting on some blue plastic gloves and giving me some, too. His anger magically changed to excitement and he started bouncing up and down.

'Watch me,' he said. And he lifted up the cow pat and sent all these flies buzzing around. Underneath, the poo was wet and smelt so bad, I had to hold my nose. But inside were worms and maggots, squirming around like they knew they'd been caught.

Dad laughed and it made me smile wide, because I'd never seen anyone that excited about poo before. He reached in, pulled out a long worm and put it into a lunchbox.

I looked back at Rosie to see if she saw how long that worm was, but her whole face was white like a ghost and she was looking out over the field.

'Dad . . .' she croaked.

The anger lines on Dad's forehead folded back, as he sighed and said, 'Would you please just—'

But then Rosie all of a sudden jumped over the fence and threw herself at me and grabbed my cow-pat gloves in her bare hands, all the time yelling, 'RUN!'

And Dad and I looked back, both at the same time, and saw the bull running, running, running at us and sounding like a whole stampede of trains, with big bursts of steam billowing out. His horns were down and pointed at our hearts and—

We stumbled and ran and shouted and my heart jumped. And Rosie threw me over the fence, so I landed on the other side hard on my back, and she and Dad raced over after me, just as the bull pulled up and huffed this noise that sounded madder than Dad had ever been before.

We all lay there in the mud with the cow-pat worms for ages and ages until Dad said that it was time to go home. And when we walked back, we did it in silence.

We never did go fishing, which was a shame, because I bet I could've seen some wonderful birds near the river.

It's thought that jackdaws are one of the few birds that can recognize human faces

I climb back over the stile and look hard at my map, but there aren't any other footpaths except this one, unless I go far along the road in the wrong direction and loop back on myself. I really don't want to do that, because time is marching on and Rosie is still missing.

The map says to walk diagonally through the field, right through the cows. And just thinking about that is making my heart beat hard and fast, and I'm definitely panicking again.

A jackdaw flutters down next to me on the fence, looking at me sideways like she's wondering what's wrong.

'I don't think I can walk through those cows, and I don't know what to do,' I tell her. 'I need to find Rosie.'

She crows at me and takes off, flying across the field to a tree standing tall in the middle. But I can't do that because I'm just a human boy without any wings.

I hold the fence so hard that the wood starts to hurt my hands. I'm starting to feel dizzy now and it's making my eyes water. I really don't want to start crying, because then I won't be able to see if the cows start running towards me.

I open my *Book of Birds* to calm myself down with some bird facts, like Mum showed me once when she got called out to school because I'd lost my money for lunch and was panicking worse than usual. That was when Mum and Dad kept worrying about money, so my

Jackdaw

usual quick thoughts and stomach ache had turned into a leaping in my chest, making it feel really tight. She'd knelt down in front of me and put my book in my hands.

'Okay, Jasper. Let's take our mind off this with some birds, shall we?'

I read the same facts now as I did then, with Mum next to me in the school office.

JACKDAWS

A group of Italian thieves once trained a jackdaw to steal money from cash machines. Jackdaws make good thieves, because they're clever and like stealing things to make their nests look nice.

I'm reading when I hear something behind me. A lady with grey hair and a puffy black coat walks up to the stile and balances a long wooden stick on the fence.

'Are you all right, dear?'

I close the book and look at her wellies, which are caked in mud.

She points at my map. 'Have you got yourself lost?'

I want to hide my face and pretend she's not there until she walks away. But then I remember Lulu and how she told me to be brave enough to say hello, so I lift my head and sniff. 'No, I know where I am. And I know I need to get over there, across the field, so I can find my sister. It's just that the cows are in the way.'

She looks with me and throws her head back and laughs loud. The cows look more interested than ever now, and some even move slowly towards us, so I jump back from the fence.

'Now, there's nothing to be scared of,' the lady says. 'They're just inquisitive. You would be too if some strange woman and a boy started laughing outside your home.'

She laughs again. I shrink down a little bit.

'You know, I used to be terrified of birds,' she says, reading the title of the book in my hands.

I peek up at her. 'But they're not scary at all.'

She chuckles again, and I think that's probably just what she does all the time. 'I know, it was silly, wasn't it? I think I was frightened that they would fly into my face.'

I shake my head. 'They don't usually do that.'

'Exactly!' she says. 'So, do you know what I did? I bought a budgie and kept him for fifteen years. He became my very best friend and I wasn't afraid at all by the end. It was just old Madge and Birdy until the day he died.'

I scratch at the fence. 'I'm sorry about your budgie, Madge. But I don't think I have space to keep a cow at home.'

She smiles. 'No, I suppose you don't.' She points her stick into the field. 'I do though. These are my dairy cows. I hand-fed each and every one of these myself when they were babies and most of their mothers too.'

I raise my eyebrows and look at the cows again. I never thought of cows belonging to anyone before. They were just huge beasts blocking the way whenever Rosie and I went walking together. That day with the bull never bothered Rosie at all afterwards; she would just take off along the path into the cows like they weren't even there, whilst I dithered at the edge.

'Come on, Jasper!' she'd shout from the other side. 'Be brave!'

Eventually though, I'd just give up and go back home. That doesn't seem like an option this time, though.

I hold my book tightly. 'Can you move them, please?'

I ask Madge, quietly. 'My sister is waiting for me to find her.'

Madge peers across the field like she might be able to see Rosie waiting on the other side. 'Your older sister, is it? Well, how about we make a deal, then. I'll walk you across the field myself, if you say hello to my favourite cow – Brown Socks. She's as friendly as a dog, that one.'

I don't want to go into the field at all whilst the cows are there, but I don't have a choice. I suppose it would be better to walk through with someone who does it all the time.

I give Madge a small nod and she smiles kindly at me. 'Okay. There are some rules to walking in a cow field. I'll tell you them.'

<u>MADGE'S RULES FOR WALKING IN A COW FIELD</u>

1. Never, ever run. Cows love a chase and if you fall over, they struggle to stop. So take it nice and steady and watch your step.

2. If you see a cow with a baby, stay away. Some mothers can get protective, so find another route, or keep your distance from her.

3. If you're not sure, keep to the edge of the field. You can always jump in a hedge then if you need to!

I run the rules over and over in my head and clench my jaw.

Madge waves her stick. 'And don't worry. You're going in with the farmer. If any of them get too nosey, I'll shout "boo" to them and they'll all run away, the softies.'

She hops up on the stile and helps me over it too. Her hand feels scratchy and dusty in mine, but I keep hold of it even when I'm back on the grass again.

'Now, here we go,' she says, chirpily. 'Nice and slow.'

And then we're walking through the cows. As we get close, they stop chewing at the grass and lift their heads to look at us. Their tails are flicking with flies and I wonder if that means they're angry at something or are about to strike, because that's what happens with my cat Fish at home. Every time one of them moves, I jump and Madge gives my hand a little squeeze.

I'm watching a mostly-white one with black freckles because it's started to walk towards us, slowly. I pull back on Madge's hand.

'It's okay,' she says. 'Some of them are more inquisitive than others. It's probably the same with birds, is it? I always found my Birdy was very pleased to sit on my shoulder, but other birds you see fly away as soon as they see you.'

I decide there and then that I like Madge a lot. 'Robins are inquisitive. They follow people and other big things like deer around, because sometimes it means they get food.'

My panic starts to die down slightly. The cows mostly stay standing where they were as we walk by, some even going back to munching grass, like they're already bored of us.

'Here she is,' Madge says. 'Old Brown Socks.'

I look up and see a huge cow walking right towards us and some of my confidence leaks out again.

'She's lovely and friendly,' Madge says. 'Comes

over to see me whenever she can, don't you, girl?' She puts out her hand and the cow nods its head, pushing into Madge's outstretched hand and trying to suck her fingers.

I look down at the cow's hooves and see that it has brown markings up its legs – just like brown socks.

'Would you like to stroke her? She loves a good scratch just here.' Madge tickles the top of the cow's head.

I look around. I want to keep walking out of the field, so my insides can stop feeling so tight. But Brown Socks looks at me and now I'm next to her and she's not moving, I don't feel as afraid as I did. That shouldn't make sense, so maybe somehow I've got braver.

I take a deep breath and reach out my hand.

Brown Socks sniffs me, cow snot spraying on my fingers. I can't quite reach the top of her head, so I scratch her between the eyes. Her hide feels like when I haven't washed my hair in a few days and I smile.

Madge laughs and pats Brown Socks herself too, and I think the cow is enjoying all the attention. 'You know, I call this the field of lost things. I've lost all sorts of things in here over the years – a necklace; earphones; even one of these sticks. The most important though was Birdy's leg tag. He used to wear it around his foot, like how these cows have tags in their ears. And when he died, I kept it in my pocket to remember him. But this field has it hidden somewhere now.'

She looks around at the grass, like she might suddenly find it again. Brown Socks bends and starts sucking the bottom of my jumper, putting cow spit all over me. I laugh and push her away.

Madge nudges me. 'Looks like this field has taken something from you too, Jasper.' I look up at her and she smiles. 'Your fear.'

I feel embarrassed that she knew I was afraid, but I also quite like the idea that it's something I could drop, like a leg tag.

'I'm sorry you lost such an important thing,' I say, thinking about the nightingale.

She sighs, patting Brown Socks goodbye and walking me over towards the tree in the centre of the field. 'I'm sorry, too. The funny thing is that Birdy himself might have been able to find it – he was great at spotting shiny things.'

I nod at that. 'A lot of birds are. Especially ones like magpies and jackdaws.' My insides leap. 'Madge, there's a jackdaw nesting in this tree!'

She frowns and smiles at me jumping around, but I can see that she doesn't understand. So, I quickly open the *Book of Birds* and tell her the story.

The week before Rosie moved to university last September, Mum spent days and days sorting all her stuff into piles that meant they were either 'staying at home' or 'going to university'. But Rosie didn't seem to want anything at all in the 'going to university' pile. Including herself.

'Maybe I should just stay here,' Rosie said, rummaging through her box of feathers. 'My car's making a funny noise and I've lost the keys, anyway. I'll just stay here, with Jasper.'

My heart leapt up and did a somersault at that, but Mum pinched her eyes. 'Rosie. I know you're worried about leaving, but I promise you, sweetheart, it will be *fine*. Now, can you just be brave for one second and try to find your car keys? I need to get this packed before my Big Meeting.'

Mum's 'Big Meeting' was all she and Dad had been

talking about for weeks and weeks. It was the thing that was going to decide whether or not we were going to be able to get enough money to keep living in our house, so it was really important. But it was also on the day Mum was supposed to take Rosie to university.

I could tell that Mum felt really bad about not being able to drive Rosie up there and help her move into her new student house. Her eyes were red and she was trying not to look at anyone. And however much Rosie said 'it's fine' and 'I don't need help anyway', I think she was a bit upset too.

When Mum left to put the boxes into Rosie's rust-bucket car, Rosie charged over to her window.

'I'll show her what brave looks like,' Rosie muttered. She pushed the window open and lifted her bare feet on the frame and then ducked up and out, until she was standing outside and holding on to the roof of the house.

My heart whooshed and I caught her by the bottom of her trousers. 'What are you doing?!' I hissed. 'You'll fall!'

She peered down at me. 'Come on – be *brave*, Jasper. Come with me.'

She kicked her foot and I lost my grip and she was gone up, and away.

I leaned out of the window and looked up to the

bright blue sky towards the top of the roof, and saw her use all her strength to lift herself up onto the roof tiles, which clacked and rattled under her. Then I looked down and saw the tangle of garden a whole downstairs away, and my brain was chattering like teeth, because Rosies can't fly if they fall.

'Come on!' she shouted from the top of the roof.

I gripped the side of the window and I put my foot on the windowsill, but everything and the world was saying 'don't you do this, Jasper,' and 'you'll get hurt,' and my whole body started shaking.

'Rosie!' I cried out.

'You've got to be brave if you want to find birds, Jasper,' she called from somewhere far above, and I wanted to be brave too. I wanted to climb out and follow her, but I couldn't do it. So I ran away. And before I even knew, I was running down the stairs to the car, where Mum was red-faced and sweaty from loading boxes onto Rosie's feathery back seats.

'Jasper, go—'

'Rosie's on the roof!' I shouted over her.

All the colour leaked from Mum's face. She ran around the tangle of garden to the back of the house, where we could see Rosie with her head in the chimney pot.

'Get down here right now!' Mum yelled, shaking like she was climbing out of the window herself.

Rosie popped her head up, smiling. 'Hey, Mum – I've found a jackdaw nest!'

Mum boiled over like hot milk and her words were frothy. 'Rosie! Rosie – get down. Get down right now or I'll – I'll . . .'

But Rosie didn't come down. She stayed looking at the jackdaw on the roof, and the panic Mum was feeling started leaking into my panic, and soon it was difficult to breathe and I could see spots.

It felt like I was falling into a deep, black sea, with only Mum's hand to hold on to.

'Jasper? Jasper, it's okay, it's okay. I'm here,' Mum said through the storm.

And Rosie heard that. She climbed off the roof without Mum or me even noticing and was there on the ground suddenly – safe and sound – crouched in front of me and dangling her car keys.

'Hey – Jasper? Don't worry. I've found my keys. The jackdaw must have taken them.'

And I could hear Mum scoffing that a jackdaw would never have managed to take a set of car keys that high, but the story calmed me down like I was climbing off my own roof, until I was on solid ground and breathing normally again.

I don't know if Rosie did find her car keys in the nest, or if they were just in her pocket all along. But whatever she found up on the roof – it was enough to finally start her car and drive away.

The collective noun for jackdaws is a 'clattering' or a 'train'

I close the book. It's strange that I read that whole story out, because I get really nervous reading things in class and I know the others at school much better than I know Madge. Maybe the field really has taken away my fear.

I peer up at Madge and see that she has her hand over her heart. 'You were definitely right not to jump out of that window, dear – goodness me! Maybe I was wrong – a bit of fear I think can be a good thing, don't you?'

But I shake my head. 'I wasn't being brave. But anyway, don't you see? Jackdaws steal things for their nests.' I look up at the tree. 'And there's a jackdaw nesting in this tree. Can you hear her?'

We're silent until we can hear the *jack-jack* crow of the bird, coming from the top of the branches above.

'Well, if Birdy's leg tag is all the way up there, then I'll never get it back,' Madge sighs.

I smile shyly at her. 'I climb trees all the time with Rosie. I can get it for you.'

I pass Madge my bag and my book as she shakes her head. 'I'm not sure you should be following your sister's lead there, dear; she's a bit of a risk-taker that one, is she?'

My stomach does a little flip, but I shake my head until it steadies itself. 'Rosie is brave and you have to be brave if you want to find things.' I look up at the branches. 'You have to do everything you can.'

I jump high and catch the lowest branch, hooking my legs around it.

'I really don't think . . .' Madge says nervously, but I show her that I'm fine by pulling myself up and crouching on the branch. I dust my hands together and reach to get the next branch. And the next. The tree is almost like a ladder. There's no branch-bench in the middle of this tree like the one back home, but the more I climb, the more I feel like I'm back there with Rosie, listening to the nightingale.

I look out and see the sky like a pond, with ratted clouds clogging up the surface. I can see birds flying and a plane sketching lines in the sky, and it all looks like a painting that I've been drawn into.

I look up and I can see a hole in the tree just a few branches above me.

'Be careful!' Madge calls, and I am.

The branches get thinner and thinner, and I need to be extra-careful not to tangle myself up in them and to have a strong place to stand.

Eventually, I reach it. And I'm out of breath from the climb but smiling wide when the jackdaw flutters out of the hole, a bit alarmed to see me all the way up there.

I look at the jackdaw in the black-bead eye. She looks even more beautiful from all the way up here, where the sun is so close that it's almost singeing her feathers.

I peer inside the hole. There are four spotted eggs in the nest and I suddenly feel a twist of guilt at disturbing her from it. What wasn't in the story in the *Book of Birds* was how bad Rosie felt after being on the roof – both for making me panic more than I've ever panicked before, and for accidentally disturbing the jackdaw in her chimney nest in her excitement. I sometimes forget to put the bad parts of a story in, as I only like to remember the good things with happy endings. But the truth is that disturbing a bird's nest is illegal and not a very nice thing to do.

I bite my lip. I want to help Madge, but I don't want to hurt the jackdaw and her nest. I look at the nest again, and see quite a few things in there:

A pheasant tail feather
A silver necklace
A pair of tangled earphones
A sweet packet
A small green bird tag

My heart whooshes. It would be very easy to lean in and get the leg tag, so Madge could be happy again. I

81

don't even think the jackdaw would mind much, as it's not soft or warm.

I look at the jackdaw, looking at me like I'm a predator after her eggs. And suddenly, I don't want to be up the tree any more. The only reason Rosie and I love to find birds in the first place is to help them stay safe. Sometimes, it's easy to forget that in our excitement to find them.

I quickly climb away from the nest, so the jackdaw can hop back in and check on her eggs.

I say sorry to the jackdaw before climbing down and Madge laughs loudly when I tell her that I found Birdy's leg tag, but left it in the nest anyway.

'You did the right thing. The leg tag was only special to me because Birdy was. My memories are all up here.' She taps the side of her head.

I still feel bad. 'I said I'd find it for you, though.'

'But, Jasper, you did! And now I'll know exactly where it is every time I come into the field, and I thank you for that. But nothing is ever as important as your health and well-being, you remember that.'

I nod. I still want to help Madge, as she helped me, so I bend and find an ink-black jackdaw feather hidden in the grass. 'It's not Birdy's, I know, but it's the jackdaw's,'

I say. 'I don't think she'll mind you keeping that.'

She smiles and hugs the feather to her chest, tight.

As we reach the gate at the other side of the cow field, Madge peers closely at me. 'Is your sister far? She is meeting you, isn't she? I'm not sure you should be walking on your own.'

I want to ignore the question, but Madge has been really kind to me. But I also know that a lot of adults don't understand that Rosie and I are fine on our own, so I choose my words carefully, so I don't technically tell her any lies.

'Don't worry – Rosie and I walk together all the time. She's eighteen, so she's an adult now.'

Madge still doesn't seem sure. 'You're meeting her soon, are you?'

I don't have to lie at all about that one. 'Really soon!' I beam at her. 'Thanks for everything, Madge.'

'You take care of yourself!' she calls as I walk away.

I'm actually feeling good about my search for Rosie, now I've shown how good I am at finding things. First it was Buster, and then it was Birdy's leg ring, and it won't be long now until I'm back listening to the nightingale with my sister in a tree, with everything back to normal again. I just know it.

I look at my watch and see that it's three o'clock already. I'm not sure where the time is going, but I'm starting to worry that I won't get to the service station before it gets dark. And the thought of Rosie there all by herself at night is worrying.

There are other questions hiding with that one. Like how Rosie would have been there for a whole week of nights, or why her phone is off when it's usually always on. They're questions that make me start to panic again, when I've been doing such a good job being brave. I push them as far down in my mind as they can possibly go, and take out my own phone instead.

It's almost completely empty of battery now and I have a lot of missed calls from Mum, which probably hasn't helped. I quickly Google 'what time does the sun set today?' before it shuts down altogether.

The results say that it's not until 20:42, so I have ages yet. But then my phone flashes an empty battery symbol at me and turns itself off before I can listen to any of the messages from Mum anyway, which I'm secretly pleased about.

She's probably just mad at me for taking the ten pounds for the bus, or for not telling her that I was leaving – that's all. It's not really my fault though. If they didn't shut the door to the study, or just listened to me when I needed to tell them something important, then maybe they could have come with me. Maybe they could even have given me a lift, so I wouldn't have had to take the money for the bus in the first place, or walk all this way.

Rosie is always mad at them for working. Whenever she's home, she shouts at them for not looking after me properly, and they shout at her for 'poisoning my mind against them'. All of it makes me tired. Sometimes, it's just better if Mum and Dad stay locked in their study forgetting about us. Rosie is always there for me and listens to me. And now, I'm going to be there for her, too.

I'm going to find her.

I keep walking. The path sends me up a steep hill, and I have to put my hands on my knees to push myself. My breath sounds huffy like an engine when I make it to the top. It's a nice view though. One side of the hill is chock-full of bright yellow plants that make it look like it's on fire. And on the other, there's the road the bus would have gone down and then a whole patchwork of fields that meet a blue line in the distance that I think is the sea.

A seagull flies over me, hardly even moving its wings.

Rosie told me once that birds can fly on things called 'thermals', which is like a wind that goes up and down. It must be like living on an invisible rollercoaster only you can see, only you get to control what bits go up and down and loop-the-loop.

I lift my head up to the sky and put my arms out too, to pretend that I'm flying with it. And I think I can feel the thermals blowing between my feather fingers lifting me up, high. It makes me feel like I could be anywhere and anything. And I know in my bones what I want to be, and where I want to go and that is with Rosie.

All I need to do to see her is keep flying.

BIRD FACT #12

Birds have hollow bones that help them fly

I've been walking for miles.

I walked through the yellow flower field, which made my nose itch and my eyes water. I hacked my way through a bridle path that was overgrown with brambles which scratched at my clothes. And I ran all the way around the outside of a football pitch, because I saw a pheasant that looked just like the one the bus hit, and I wanted to make sure it was okay. It was a bit worried about me following it, but it was fine.

My boots are hurting now and are pinching like crabs at my heels. The clouds have also started gathering up in a team and are turning into something that looks angry, so I put my coat on and keep walking as fast as I can along the paths, until my back is sweaty and my bag is feeling heavy, even though I've drunk all my water.

I climb over a gate and into a tiny village the map says is called Scatterton. It's nice to see a few shops and people after all those miles on my own. The road is busy, and people keep pulling up on the pavement in their cars to nip into the post office and the chip shop.

The chips smell amazing. So amazing actually, that I look both ways and cross the road to stick my face up against the window. My stomach rumbles. There's a queue almost to the door, mainly made up of men who are standing looking at their phones, or trying to see into the glass case at the front to view the different types of fish and sausages and pies.

One man comes out with his chips open in a polystyrene tray with a wooden fork in the top, and they look so good. Rosie would say that they look the perfect amount of crispy and soggy, which is a very fine balance and difficult to find.

I still have six pounds in my pocket. I want to go in and see how many chips I could get for that, but I should save it for when I see Rosie at the service station. I'd like to buy her some chips to say sorry for taking so long to get to her. I still have two seedy-nut bars and a chocolate bar in my bag that I can eat instead, although I've run out of water now, which probably isn't very good.

I leave the window and the chip smell and head to the post office next door, which says it closes at 5.30 p.m. and it's 5.25 p.m. now. There are a few people in the queue, so I nip over to the fridge in the corner to look at the drinks. I want to buy a big bottle of water, but it's two pounds! There is a carton of juice though for ninety pence, so I pick that instead and pay for it at the counter.

'Do you have anything for ten pence?' I ask, as I hand the lady behind the till a pound coin.

She shakes her head and hands my change back to me and I suppose that's that. I still have my drink at least, though.

I open the door again and stop still. Outside, it has started to rain. I step back out of the way, and wear my bag on my front, so I can zip it under my coat. I don't have anything to keep my legs dry, and I wonder if that's going to be a problem.

I walk back into the post office and sink down to the floor in a corner next to the envelopes and I drink my drink. It reminds me of the cartons you get at school, which feels like a million miles away from where I am now. Sitting in a corner on my own feels familiar, though.

It's not that I don't have friends at school. I play football at lunchtimes, and I'm quite good – I've scored loads of goals. But as soon as we're in the classroom, everyone seems to have a best friend group, and I don't feel like I fit anywhere. Speaking to them always makes me worry that they won't understand me – not like Rosie does. I know none of them like birds or wildlife as much as I do. And so I usually just go off on my own, because it's easier that way.

I slurp my drink and think about what Lulu said, about being brave enough to say hello. I've managed to talk more than I ever usually do to her and to Madge today. Maybe if I plucked up the courage to speak to more people in my class, I might find that we could be friends after all – just like I hope Lulu and Madge and I might be friends now.

The last customer leaves the shop and the woman at the till comes around to the door and gives a little jump when she sees me.

'What on earth . . . ? Come on – out. We're closing.'

'But it's raining,' I say, standing up.

'You should have spent your money on an umbrella then, shouldn't you?'

She holds the door open for me and I can hear the water coming down quite fast now. I want to tell her that it says that umbrellas are eight pounds and I don't have enough for that. Or that she should try taking the time to listen too, so she can make more friends.

But I don't, because she seems angry at me. I just put my hood up and my head down and I walk out into the rain, up the road, and into the next field.

BIRD FACT #13

Most birds are waterproof, thanks to naturally occurring oils they coat their feathers with

When it rains heavily like it's doing now, a lot of birds will hide in bushes and trees, and sit snuggled up and still until it stops.

I can't do that because I need to find Rosie, so I keep walking.

Rosie told me once about something called 'hypothermia', which is where your body leaks out its heat and you get really cold. She told me about it, because people who go on adventures like we do can get it, so you have to be careful. I make sure that I stick my hands in my pockets and keep my coat done up, and I make a note to change my socks as soon as I can find somewhere dry.

I go around some big farm buildings and wonder if I can duck into some of those, but they're full of pigs that are making sounds like aliens. The soggy map says I need to walk between two of the big sheds, but the path is a whole river of water now.

When we first started going on adventures, Rosie told me how important it was to stick to the footpaths on the map, so you don't accidentally trespass and do something illegal. But it's raining and cold and the pigs are making my chest feel fluttery, so I turn and run through a barn towered up to the roof with straw bricks. I run fast and try to keep my head down, but the wind roars through a hole in the roof and it sounds like a farmer shouting at me like I'm a wanted criminal.

I run and run, and even though the sunset isn't for ages yet, it's started to get quite dark and I can feel the panic getting worse.

I can't read the *Book of Birds* to make me feel better, because the pages would get wet. But I can remember the most recent story I wrote in it, when Rosie drove back from university last time and told me about a crow she'd seen on her car before she left.

She was describing its petrol-black feathers and beady eyes, and I thought it was amazing that she'd got so close to it, when she told me that it was dead. Its wings were bent at funny angles and it wasn't breathing any more, and she thought that maybe it had fallen out of a tree during the night and died.

'I don't like this story,' I said, quietly.

Rosie stopped describing its little body and put her arm around me on the sofa.

'That's the circle of life though, Jasper. If all crows got to live for ever, then there wouldn't be enough insects for them to eat, would there? And the crow's body won't go to waste now it's dead – it will help feed hundreds and hundreds of insects.'

Her eyes were bright and smiling, but I wriggled away. 'Crows aren't the same as maggots though, Rosie.

Maggots are disgusting and crows are beautiful and magic.'

She shrugged. 'All life is life, Jasper. Just because one creature is small, it doesn't mean it's got any less right to be alive. That maggot would turn into a fly, that would keep other birds alive, those birds would maybe even get eaten by other animals, and it's been like that for millions of years.'

I don't like that story very much, so I don't know why I'm thinking about it now. I scrunch the rainwater from my eyes and try to think about Rosie when we were up in our tree and holding hands and listening to the nightingale singing. And how I didn't just hear it, but could see the notes exploding in my eyes like fireworks, and crackling over my skin, like I had a song all of my own that was just waiting to burst out and turn the whole world to silence. But it's difficult to remember that, when all I can hear and feel and see is rain.

I finally get away from the farm to a little stream, and follow it along as it chatters over sharp rocks. It runs along the backs of some gardens that are long and thin, and joined up by the same footpath. I feel strange being in someone's garden who I don't know, but can't keep checking the map in the rain to make sure it's not trespassing.

And then above, something rumbles, low and throaty, like a woodpecker vibrating the sky, and I see a huge flash and freeze.

There's a tree on the other side of the stream, but everyone knows that is the worst place to stand in a thunderstorm, as the lightning might strike and it could fall on you. So I take off, running into one of the gardens instead, the rain pecking at my hood and dripping off my nose and spraying up out of the grass at my feet. I run until I see a garden shed, and wishing with all my might that it isn't locked, I put my hand on the handle and it opens as I turn.

Throwing myself inside, I clatter right over a spade, which falls into a tower of flowerpots, and I tumble with them onto the floor, which hurts quite a lot. And I think it's the rain and the hurt of falling over and also the relief of not being out in the storm any more, but I can't stop it.

I stuff myself into a corner of the shed and cry.

Water helps keep a bird's body cool on the inside and the outside

The rain goes on and on and on. And soon the sun goes down and it gets really dark.

The later it gets, the more worried I feel. I was supposed to have found Rosie ages ago, but now I'm stuck on my own in a strange place. I can't give up and go back home, because then I might never find Rosie and that thought is unthinkable. But I also can't keep walking all through the night in a thunderstorm.

I stand on a table in the corner of the shed and look through a small window at the top towards a dark house further up the garden. There might be someone in there who'd be able to help me, but the thought of knocking on the door is even scarier than being struck by lightning.

I climb down again and look around. At least in here I'm warm and safe. If I don't think about it too much, it's almost like camping, and I know how to do that, thanks to all the times Rosie has taken me camping in the garden.

I use my wind-up torch as a light and take off my wet things, hanging them up on the rake and the spade inside the shed to dry off. Dad was right, it is always useful to carry a towel. It feels good to put some clean socks on, and I find a jumper stuffed in a bucket that smells old and probably has spiders in it, but it's warm when I put it on and goes almost all the way to my knees.

I eat one of the seedy-nut bars, and then the other. I was going to save the chocolate biscuit bar for emergencies, but I'm still hungry and upset, so I eat that too.

When I used to get upset, Mum would climb into bed with me and stroke my hair until I fell asleep. Sometimes we even watched cartoons on her phone. And Dad would bring my dinner up to my room for me and we'd eat all together in bed.

But now all they do is work – even since Mum's 'Big Meeting' went well and they saved the house, so they shouldn't need to work so much. But they still eat their dinners in their study whilst on the phone and leave mine out on the side with a note saying 'sorry' or 'it's just for tonight', but it never is.

Before they started their business, they weren't like that at all. I even remember two years ago when it was Rosie's sixteenth birthday, they were both around for the whole day and it felt like we were living in a Christmas card, where everything was perfect.

The only thing she wanted for her birthday that year was a wildlife hide. We'd seen some at the Wildlife Centre on one of our adventures, and they were like little sheds with a long bench and a window, which you could hide in to watch birds. They were great, because animals like birds can be nervous about people watching them sometimes, so hides make them feel safer about coming out of the bushes.

Rosie didn't think Mum and Dad were going to get her a hide, because they were big and expensive and take a lot of time to put together. They were also about birds and Dad has never understood why we like birds so much. He feels like we're too obsessed with them, which is funny when you think about it, because he talks about his seedy-nut bar business all the time.

But they bought one for her.

Dad woke up early and laid all the pieces out on the floor, like a jigsaw of wood and bags of nails and bolts. And after breakfast, Dad put his glasses on and hunched over the instructions like he does with his laptop, but instead of telling us to go away and leave him in peace, he was telling us to help him hammer bits of wood together with nails.

The hide went up higher and higher and higher, and at midday, Mum came out with trays of cheese sandwiches and hot chips, which are Rosie's favourites.

And as we were working, Rosie was telling us all

kinds of facts about wildlife hides, and badgers, and rabbits and even birds, and Dad was just listening and humming and even smiling. He didn't shout or tell her to be quiet. And when he spoke about the seedy-nut bars, Rosie even listened to him and came up with a new idea for their website.

When it was done, the hide looked wonky and there were a lot of nails left over, which I didn't know if there should be, but we had built it together and Rosie said that made it the best wildlife hide in the world. Mum came out with hot chocolates made with real milk and not water – which she never does, because it takes too long to make – and we all crammed in the hide together and sat in a line on the bench, looking out of the window.

We waited and we watched for ages, but we didn't see a single thing. But it was okay, because we were together without anyone shouting, and it was probably one of the last times I remember that happening.

This shed isn't as nice as our wildlife hide. It smells like the jumper I found – old and dusty. There's no bench to sit on with your family, and the small window at the top isn't letting in much light because it's too dark outside now.

Remembering the story has made me miss Mum and Dad a bit, which used to happen a lot when I was younger, but doesn't happen as much any more. I suppose I got used to them being too busy. I have missed them extra-hard this week though, maybe because things have been so strange. I keep catching Dad sitting in Rosie's room, crying. Or Mum staring blankly out of the window, like she's not seeing anything at all.

My insides feel twisted up. Now I've thought about them I feel guilty – like perhaps I shouldn't have gone out. I know I left a note, but I have a feeling Mum won't like not being able to tuck me in tonight and they're probably worried about me.

Sometimes, when feelings are really complicated and painful, I try to ignore them. That's what Dad always says when I'm panicking.

'Try not to worry, Jasper. Distract yourself with some good things.'

A good thing is that I really am safe in this shed. And even though I'm not there yet, it feels like by staying here, I'm finally doing something good and useful rather than sitting around at home, not going to school. As soon as it's morning, I'm going to keep trying to find Rosie's Better Place, and that thought makes me feel brave.

I know if Dad were here, he'd have tips for camping out, too, because he was a Boy Scout once upon a time. I bet he'd have a good idea for how I could get a drink.

The rain whips up outside and it's like I can hear Dad in my ear telling me what to do. I pick up my empty drink bottle and find a funnel in the shed that only looks a little bit dirty. Then, I open the door, dig the bottle as far as I can into the ground so it doesn't fall over, and balance the funnel in the top. I watch it for a bit, as the rain falls into the funnel and then drips into the bottle, filling it up slowly.

It'll take a while to have enough to drink though, so I come back inside to lie down on the towel in the corner, using my coat as a duvet and an old deflated ball I find hidden under a bucket as a pillow.

I stay awake for ages – later than I've ever been awake before. But the rain is hammering nails on the shed roof and just thinking about Rosie still being lost is making my stomach ache again.

I try to turn my phone on again to call her, but it's wet as well as out of battery now. I send out a mind-message to her though.

'I'm sorry for taking so long, Rosie,' I whisper. 'I'm doing my best.'

BIRD FACT #15

Many artists have been inspired by the song of the nightingale

I'm dreaming that I'm walking through a forest in the dark. The forest isn't like Springy Wood that I walked through earlier, but is thick with bushes and branches and bracken, and thorny things keep getting caught on my hood and pulling me back.

And I'm walking and walking, but not getting very far at all.

And then I hear it.

'Jasper!'

It's a bird call, but I understand it and know that it's my sister, too.

'Rosie!' I call out. I spin round and try to see her, and suddenly I have night-vision and see her ahead of me, tangled and lost. And she is a nightingale, and she's fluttering and her breast is caught on a thorn.

'Stay there, I'm coming!' I shout.

I try to move forwards, but now vines are snaking around my feet and spiky bushes are in my way and it's getting harder to move. I push and I push even though it hurts.

'I'm coming, Rosie!' I shout again.

But I'm not. If anything, I'm getting further and further away. I can see her struggling against the thorns and I wish that she wouldn't move, because she only has a little heart as a nightingale and I don't want her song to leak out.

Then suddenly, she breaks free and takes flight, and the trees turn to feathers and stop hurting me any more.

But instead of being happy that she is finally flying away, I reach my hand out through the feathers and scream at her to come back.

Come back.

Don't leave me behind on my own.

It's thought that most birds see humans as potential predators

Waking up feels like climbing a huge mountain wearing a backpack full of rocks.

For a moment, I think that I'm back home in my bed. I wonder if Mum will be calling me soon for breakfast, or telling me that I'm late for school again. But then I open my eyes and remember that I'm sleeping on an old football on the floor of someone's shed and the light through the window at the top is pouring in like milk, making everything white.

I blink. I can't belive that I made it through the night all on my own in a shed in the middle of a thunderstorm. My heart leaps up and I feel proud and brave and also anxious that Mum and Dad might be worried about me and I've got no way of telling them that I'm fine.

I lean over to feel my trousers that I left hanging up. They're almost dry now, so I put them on and take the old shed-jumper off.

My stomach grumbles loudly as it wakes up. I was silly last night eating all the leftover food, when all that's in this shed is probably just spiders and there's no way I'm eating those. But at least I have the water.

I crawl over to the door and inch it open. The grass is looking lime-green today, like it doesn't even know what rain is because it's such a nice day. My water bottle is half-full of water from last night though, and I drink it all fast in one gulp. It tastes a bit funny, but it's nice to have something to drink.

I sit back on my knees and wipe my mouth. And then

a shadow passes over me and says in a suspicious voice:

'What are you doing in my dad's shed?'

I shout in surprise and throw the water bottle at the voice without thinking.

'Hey!' the shadow says, ducking out of the way.

My heart is beating in my ears as I scramble to my feet, ready to leave everything I own behind in the shed and run away as fast as I can. But then I see that the shadow isn't a monster, but a dark-haired boy wearing a stripy football top.

It should probably be less scary to see someone who looks my own age rather than a monster, but it isn't. It just makes me feel the same worry I do at school and I retreat back into the shed, trying to shut the door on him.

'Hey,' he says again, stopping the door from closing. 'You can't just break in here, you know. My dad needs all this stuff . . .' He trails off, sadly.

I quickly pack my things into my bag and stomp on my boots, without stopping to do them up. 'I'm sorry – I didn't mean to break in. It's just that there was a storm and I was worried I'd get electrocuted.'

I stand up and try to push past him out of the door, but he blocks it with his hand, a frown creasing his nose.

110

'Have you been here all night?'

I look at yesterday's mud on my boots and the boy ducks down with me, trying to see my face. I try to avoid his eye, but his frown turns into a huge, excited grin.

'Oh!' he shouts, clapping his hands together like he's just found buried treasure. 'You're that missing kid from the news!'

I snap my head up and step back, so my back is against the splintery shed walls. 'What? No – I'm not missing, I'm here.'

But the boy is nodding, scrambling in his pockets for something. 'Yeah, here in our shed! This is so cool . . .'

He pulls out his mobile phone and sticks his tongue out in concentration as he types something on the screen. I'm feeling a bit sick again. Different thoughts flap around my head, but the one I hear the loudest is that I really need to go. It's a whole new day now, and I still haven't found Rosie. And I really don't want this strange boy to see me panicking about that.

I step to push past the boy, just as he turns his phone and sticks it right in my face. The screen is bright in the dark, dusty shed and it's too close up to read properly, but I can see my own school picture staring back at me.

THE DAILY NEWS
POLICE SEARCH FOR MISSING 9-YEAR-OLD BOY

Sussex police are leading the search for missing 9-year-old Jasper Wilde, who left his home around 11 a.m. yesterday on a walk alone and didn't return.

Jasper is wearing cream walking trousers, a grey jumper and possibly carrying a red coat with blue buttons, as well as a blue school bag.

It's believed that Jasper is an experienced walker and may be sighted on countryside paths, or in popular bird-watching areas. He was last seen alone at Scatterton Post Office at 5:32 on Saturday evening.

Police say that Jasper may be distressed about his sister, who tragically—

My insides lurch at that last word and I shut my eyes tight, quickly throwing the phone at the boy, like I did with the bottle.

'Ow!' he says, catching it, just before it drops and smashes on the floor. 'What are you—?'

But there's a buzzing in my ears now and I can't be here a moment longer. Ducking under his arm, I push open the door and run as fast as possible down his garden. I skid over the grass, which is so wet that there's a huge puddle waiting at the bottom as wide as a pond. But I don't slow down and my boots aren't done up and suddenly, the ground slips under my feet and I fall, splashing into the water.

'Jasper Wilde!' the boy shouts behind me.

I'm cold and wet and in a puddle. The shock of falling over thunders like a storm cloud inside me.

And I panic.

Song thrushes are one of the few birds in Britain that eat snails

I'm breathing like I did when Rosie was on the roof looking at the jackdaw nest – like there isn't enough air in the world and I can't swallow it fast enough.

My hands grasp out and the puddle is a black sea

Song thrush

I'm drowning in, but instead of finding nothing at all – I find the hand of the boy.

I expect him to start laughing at me, but he doesn't. He bends down, even though I'm still in the puddle and now he is too, and he looks me in the eyes like he's the only steady thing in a world that's falling apart.

'It's okay,' he says. 'You're okay, just breathe with me. My name's Gan Tran-Stevens and I'm here.'

He sounds strangely like a grown-up all of a sudden and I don't believe him. My breathing is getting more gaspy and my hands are struggling and I don't like it and I'm afraid.

'You're having a panic attack,' Gan says, calmly. 'Have you had one before?'

I'm not sure and I don't know, so I shake my head and nod it all at once.

'They don't feel so good, but they're normal. You feel like you're not breathing properly, and you feel dizzy and like your heart is beating really fast – but it's okay. It's all normal and soon it'll pass and you'll feel better again.'

I feel all of those things – just like he said. And I cling to his eyes and it looks like he's telling me the truth, so I start to trust him.

'You want to hear the rules for staying calm in a panic attack? My therapist taught me all of them and they're really helpful.'

I nod and hold his hand tighter.

GAN'S RULES FOR A PANIC ATTACK

1. Keep telling yourself that you're fine, because you are. Everything you're feeling is normal and you'll be okay again soon.

2. Breathe in through your nose for three seconds, then try to hold your breath for two seconds. Then breathe out of your mouth. This is a way to help slow your breathing down.

3. Try to think only true facts and things that make you feel happy.

I count my breaths in and out with Gan. At first, I feel embarrassed but he still isn't laughing at me, so I think about true facts instead, like how the oldest known wild albatross is seventy years old, and how I'll feel better again soon – just like I did last time I felt like this, when Rosie was on the roof.

In, one, two, three. Hold. Out, one, two, three.

In, one, two, three. Hold. And out, one, two, three.

When my breathing is less raspy and I'm just hiccupping and tired, Gan helps me up. He puts my arm over his shoulder and lets me lean on him as we walk up the garden to an old, rickety bench close to the shed.

I try to say 'thank you' and 'I'm sorry', but he shoves my head between my legs.

'Don't talk, silly. Just breathe. It's okay.'

I feel better with my head lower down – like there's more air nearer the floor. I look at the insects on the ground as I count my breaths. There are ants walking in a line and a worm sliming in the grass. As I breathe, a song thrush hops onto the grass not far away, looks at us on the bench and flies away with a snail.

I close my eyes and think about facts I know about song thrushes.

FACTS ABOUT SONG THRUSHES

Song thrushes sometimes sing after dark, which means they're sometimes confused with nightingales.
They're much more common in most of the UK than nightingales though and sing all year round.

Gan shifts on the bench next to me. 'I have panic attacks sometimes, too,' he says. 'That's how I know the rules on what to do when they happen. Especially since my dad . . .'

I slowly lift my head up to look at him. I've never met anyone who worries like I do. But here is a boy my own age, clearly wondering about telling me his own story, and just like me, I can tell he's a bird that has a song he's too nervous to sing out loud.

Gan bites his lip and takes a deep breath. 'My dad went away last month. He moved with his other family to America. He promised me that I can go visit him soon, but sometimes it feels like I've lost him for ever.

It makes me feel bad sometimes – panicky, but also angry and guilty a bit.' His ears flush pink. 'The worst time was the week after he left. I took the really expensive football he bought me for my birthday that was signed by my favourite player and I kicked it so hard, I lost that, too.' He says that part really fast, and then looks relieved as well as a bit surprised that he said it at all. 'I've not told anyone about that before.'

It's a sad story, so I move closer to him on the bench, so he knows that I'm there, like he was there for me. 'He's probably not lost for ever,' I say. 'Just in a different place.' I feel for the corners of the *Book of Birds* in my bag behind me. 'It's the same with our nightingale. We used to have five or six males fly to the field behind our house when I was small, and then there was only one. And then this year, he didn't come back at all.'

My thoughts get jumbled for a moment and I shake my head until they're back to normal.

'But my sister is the best at finding birds and she's found it at the motorway services. Even though you'd think a nightingale wouldn't ever go there, next to all that traffic. I've spent ages worrying about it, but you see – it's not lost after all. It's just in a different place I haven't seen yet.'

Gan's eyes are wide. 'How do you know it's the same bird?'

'Well . . .' My back prickles and I feel hot, so I take my bag off. 'I just know.'

Gan doesn't say anything for a moment. I can hear the song thrush in the tree, pretending to be a nightingale, but not fooling me.

'If I could walk to America, I think I'd do that, too,' he says, quietly. 'I can see why you ran away from home, now.'

'I haven't run away. I don't know why that article said that . . .'

If Gan's phone didn't have my picture and my name on, I wouldn't have believed that article was about me at all. How can I be missing, when I've been the one finding things? I found Buster and Birdy's leg ring – even though I left it where it was. And now I've found a boy who says he gets anxious sometimes, just like I do.

Gan shrugs, looking at the small house at the top of the garden. 'Maybe your parents are worried about you. My mum worries a lot about me, too. It's quite annoying.'

I shake my head. 'I thought it would be okay if I left a note. That's what Rosie and I usually do . . .'

I feel awful about making Mum and Dad worry

about me so much. They used to worry about me like that when I was small. They'd tell Rosie that I was too young to go on adventures with her and I hated it. But Rosie would always sneak me out with her anyway, sometimes cleaning off the mud from my trousers before we got back in the house, but sometimes forgetting. She always did such a good job of looking out for me and we always got back safely together, so eventually Mum and Dad stopped worrying about it so much.

I think about that newspaper article again and that scary word pings into my brain: *Tragically*. It has giant wings and sharp claws, so I push it right back out of my head, standing up, fast.

'Thanks for helping me,' I say, quickly. 'But I need to go now.'

Gan stands as I do my shoelaces up. 'Go? But I just found you. I know you want to find your bird, but don't you want some food or something? Maybe you can help me find my football and then we can go tell my mum that you're here – she'll be back from the shops soon.'

At the word 'food', my stomach grumbles loudly and Gan grins.

I look at the sun, high in the sky. 'Maybe just some quick breakfast . . .'

Gan laughs, jumping and running up towards his house, so water splashes out from the grass under his trainers. 'Breakfast? Jasper Wilde, it's gone midday. More like lunch!'

My heart jumps at that. How is it so late? I know I didn't sleep very well and it took ages to wake up, but I don't think I've ever slept in past morning before. I do feel tired though. My legs hurt from all the walking yesterday and a part of me just wants to curl up back in the shed and go to sleep again.

But then Gan runs back down the hill to me, a tea tray of crisps and fruit and water bottles rattling with his footsteps.

'I got everything we had!' he says, dropping the tray between us on the bench.

I snatch a packet of cheese and onion crisps and stuff a fistful into my mouth. My stomach shouts greedily, but as soon as I finish the packet, I feel a lot better. I open another one and a banana and drink down almost a whole water bottle in one gulp.

'You should be in an eating contest – you're sucking that up like a vacuum cleaner,' Gan says.

I smile shyly at him. 'I'm really hungry. I feel like I could eat a whole shed full of crisps.'

'Not my dad's shed, you couldn't – not unless your favourite flavour is salt-and-spider.'

I laugh. 'Ready cobwebbed?'

Gan laughs so hard that he almost falls off the bench. 'Good one!'

I smile wide and feel like I have so much energy all of a sudden that I could run all the way to Rosie. And some of that is the food, and some of it is that I'm making jokes with Gan like it's the most normal thing in the whole world – even though it isn't. Not for me.

I wipe my fingers down my top, trying to think of what else was in the shed that I could make a funny new crisp name from, when I gasp. 'Gan! Your missing football . . .'

I turn round to the shed, brushing crisp crumbs off my lap, and Gan follows my eyes.

'Yeah, I was going to look in the shed this morning when I found you. I've looked everywhere else in the world, it seems. I thought maybe my mum found it and put it in there, although I don't know why she wouldn't have told me.'

I nod, running back to the door. 'I think I saw it last night. I used it as a pillow.'

I can hear Gan following me as I open the door, clatter over the same spade I did last night and find the deflated ball still where I left it.

'Is it there? Did you find it?' Gan says, excitedly.

I don't turn round right away. The football looks sad, like it's been punched in the belly. I wonder if I can quickly blow it back up again, but it's one of those posh footballs and I don't think even the biggest bird would have the lungs to do that.

'I'm sorry,' I say, as I hand it to him.

I watch his face. For a moment, he looks confused. And then his eyes turn sad and I'm sorry for making them do that. 'Oh . . .' he says. 'Was it like this when you found it last night?'

'Yes,' I say quickly, so he doesn't think I popped his ball. 'Maybe it's a different one?'

He steps outside into the light and turns it in his hand until we see a black scribble on the side from his favourite football player.

He sniffs. 'It's broken.'

I put my hand around his shoulder. He's a bit taller than I am, so I have to stand on my toes slightly. I'm not sure what to say to make him feel better, but then I think of Madge. 'You found it though. At least you know where it is now.'

He smiles sadly at me. 'Yeah. Thanks, Jasper Wilde.

I suppose it's better to know, isn't it? Even if the thing that you need to know isn't very nice.' He wipes his face on his football top. 'At least now I can stop looking.'

The sun moves from behind a cloud and I suddenly feel hot in my jumper.

We're quiet for a moment. Gan is looking awkwardly at me, like he wants to say something else, and I suddenly realize that I don't really want to listen to it.

'Jasper Wilde, I think we need to tell—'

'You can't,' I say, walking back to the bench and fetching my bag. 'I've got to go find Rosie and I'm already late. If you tell anyone else, they might stop me from finding her and I can't stop now. I can't.'

Gan scratches the back of his neck, looking at me panicking again. 'Okay . . . Maybe I can help you then, or—'

'No, thank you,' I say, quickly putting my bag on my back. 'I'm sorry again for staying in your shed. I hope everything works out with your dad!' I walk away, my ears thumping.

Gan hurries down the garden with me calling my name, uncertainly. I ignore him, looking at the toes of my boots as I splash right through the puddle I fell into earlier. And then – out of nowhere – a pair of arms grab me, spin me round and hug me tight around the middle.

I feel so shocked, I forget for a moment to hug him back. Rosie and Mum and Dad hug me all the time, but boys in my class don't. It feels nice, but also like the walls I've been building up and up in my head might fall down all of a sudden, and I don't want that. Not when I'm so close to finding her.

I wriggle away and Gan looks at me, seriously. 'Thanks for listening to me, Jasper Wilde. About my dad. I don't talk about it that much and my therapist is always going on about me sharing my feelings, but maybe I was just waiting to tell someone who understands – like you. And I know the ball was deflated, but . . .' He takes a deep breath. 'I feel better, telling you the truth about what happened.'

I nod and hide my face. And I know I should say that I'm happy he feels like that and that I'm happy I met him – because I am. But also, his words sound like high-pitched noise in my ears and I know I really need to go.

'Goodbye, Gan Tran-Stevens,' I say, using his whole name like he does with me. 'Thanks for not telling anyone that I was here!'

BIRD FACT #18

The American bittern can camouflage itself into reeds by looking skywards with its long neck and bill

I follow the rest of the path along people's gardens with my head down and my boots splashing in puddles, and I don't look up or stop until I'm spat out onto a golf course.

I don't really like walking through golf courses, as

American
Bittern

I'm always afraid that someone will accidentally hit a ball at my head, but it doesn't look like anyone is playing today. Just in case though, I walk over to the golf club building and push a bright blue door open to a small, deserted changing room that smells like old socks. It has a toilet, which I use, and then I sit on one of the benches next to some lockers and open my map.

It got a bit soggy in the rain last night, but I did at least walk the right way. And the map says it's now only one and a bit squares to where the bus would have dropped me off at Dunton Mayfield yesterday, if I hadn't run after that pheasant.

I've made it all this way, but also I'm very late. And – even worse – the article Gan showed me on his phone said that the police are after me, because they think I'm missing.

I don't like getting into trouble. Once, my teacher in Year Three shouted at me because I climbed a tree on the football field when I wasn't allowed. I still remember how angry he was and how the whole class went really silent while he shouted. It made my heart hurt from thumping so hard and sometimes I still wake up in the middle of the night, thinking about it.

This is even worse than that, as the police are

looking for me, and I'm sure they only do that for wanted criminals. Not only does everyone think I ran away, but I also trespassed on the pig farm last night when it was raining and disrupted a bird nest, which you're not allowed to do, even for a good reason like finding a budgie's leg tag.

Part of me wants to walk to the nearest police station with my head down, like I did with the teacher at school, and say sorry for making everyone mad, I didn't mean to. But also – Rosie is still missing with the nightingale. If I give up now, then both of them might stay lost for ever.

I pack the map away and take out the *Book of Birds*, opening up a page in the middle to read about the time Rosie and I went to a lake, hidden in the middle of the woods. Rosie had brought us a picnic and we'd sat all day, trying to spot water birds like moorhens and egrets with our binoculars, but only really seeing a family of mallard ducks.

'How come male birds are always so much more beautiful than the females?' I asked her, throwing a bit of my sandwich to one of the male mallards with the forest-green head feathers.

Rosie rolled her eyes. 'It depends what you mean

by beautiful, Jasper. Males usually have all the striking peacock feathers and party tricks to attract mates, but it's the females who are really the beautiful ones.'

I looked at the dull-brown feathers of the female duck in the water and wasn't sure.

'Look at it this way,' Rosie said. 'The female mallard will be the one sitting on the eggs. The male will go off somewhere with his duck pals and she'll have to protect the eggs from predators. Imagine if she had show-off feathers – the foxes would find her, no problem. But with her being the same colour as dried leaves . . .'

I looked for the female duck again, but couldn't see her any more. 'Hey, she disappeared!' I said.

And Rosie grinned. 'If you ask me, *that* is beautiful.'

Remembering that day makes me smile. We hadn't seen many different birds, but I'd learned a lot about them from Rosie teaching me about camouflage. She said all different kinds of birds from all over the world were excellent at blending into the background to protect them, or to be able to sneak up on their prey.

I'm just like one of those birds. I have people looking for me and a long way still to fly – but if I camouflage myself into the surroundings, then maybe they won't be able to see me. Maybe I can still make it.

I take everything out of my bag, looking for inspiration. If I was only walking in the wilderness, then I'd use mud and leaves to disappear into the trees. But in just over a square, I'll be walking through Dunton Mayfield, which the map shows as a grey splodge in the green, dotted with building-shapes and symbols for schools, hotels and hospitals. If I have to walk through a town like that, then I'll still need to look like a boy – just a different one.

I put on my sun hat, which hides my hair as well as my face, and then turn my school bag inside out, so it's black instead of blue. I try doing the same to my jumper and trousers too, but they're the same colour on the other side and just make me look even stranger, which I don't want. Instead, I hunt around the changing room, looking for things people might have left.

In one locker I find a roll of mints and in another I find a pair of old pants, which I close the door on again quickly. But then I walk around the locker aisles to the back, where there are different-coloured canvas bins, piled high with things.

Most of the bins are just full of towels, but another says 'lost and found'.

Rummaging through I find brightly coloured trousers

and hats, shirts that are as big as Dad's and even shoes with spiky bits on the bottom. They'd all make me stick out more, rather than blend in.

But then I find a green jumper with a logo on it saying 'Dunton Mayfield Junior Ramblers' and my insides swoop like a flock of swifts. I take my grey jumper off and although the new one smells like a dirty football kit, it fits almost perfectly.

I hunt around for some trousers, but don't find any in my size. A pair of sunglasses do a good job hiding my face though, and a white belt at least makes the top part of my trousers look different. I put it all on, turn to see myself in the mirror on the side of one of the aisles. I don't look like the Jasper Wilde from the news any more. And it makes me laugh that I lost myself in the lost and found.

I pull my inside-out bag onto my back, taking a moment to memorize as much of the map as I can, so I don't have to look at it again, and then set out with my head down – ready to sneak through town, right under everyone's noses.

Ptarmigans moult their brown feathers for white in winter to stay camouflaged in the changing weather

I'm so busy walking along the road leading away from the golf course with my head down, that I almost walk right into the sign.

WELCOME TO DUNTON MAYFIELD

It's not the finish line, but it feels like it's something huge because I made it. I made it even though the bus hit that pheasant and went without me. Even though I got caught up in a cow field and a thunderstorm. Even though the whole world is looking for me.

'I'm nearly there!' I say, out loud.

I'm so excited that I jump around like a cockatoo, with one foot up then the other. But then a car goes by me slowly – the driver peering at me from the window – and I remember that I'm supposed to be camouflaged.

Instead, I take off, running away from the road around the side of a farm with a duck pond and children throwing in loaves of bread. And I don't even stop to tell them that bread isn't actually very good for ducks and they should try throwing in peas next time, because I'm so nearly there now. And I run past cows that are safely behind fences, all the way to the front of the farm where there's a shop selling ice cream.

And I don't even stop for that, even though it's an almost perfect ice cream day and I really want one.

But not as much as I want to see Rosie.

I do stop to catch my breath eventually though, and I duck into a public toilet and into one of the stalls to check the map again. It says I need to walk around a lot of streets now, through the town, to get to the other side where the footpath leads into the countryside again, all the way to the motorway services. There are still two squares of town and five of fields to walk through until I see Rosie, but I'm feeling confident because I walked twice that yesterday.

I fold the map up again and fumble for my water bottle, before remembering that I threw it at Gan when I thought he was a monster. I should probably have stopped to put some of the food and water he got for me in my bag. I'm not hungry yet, but I'm starting to get thirsty.

I feel in my pocket for the five pounds and ten pence I have left. I think it's plenty to buy water with some still left over to buy Rosie some chips when I see her. But that means going into a shop and coming face-to-face with people.

I exit the toilet cubicle and catch myself again in the

mirror. I'm wondering if the camouflage is good enough, when the door to the toilets opens. It's a man with a beard and glasses and for a moment, I get a stomach lurch thinking that it's Dad, come to get me and take me home.

But it's not. This man is younger than my dad and he barely looks at me as he pushes past me into the toilet cubicle I just came out of – like he didn't even see me.

I catch myself in the mirror again – mouth open, not believing that my camouflage worked so well. To be sure though, I scuttle out of the door and walk quickly out of the farm car park in the middle of different families, pretending I belong to them and none of them at the same time. One by one, they reach their cars, and then it's just me.

'Hey, kid!' someone calls behind me. And I'm not sure if they're talking to me or not, but I suddenly wave at an invisible person up the road and take off, running, so they think my parents are just around the corner. My heart is thumping in my ears, expecting a hand on my shoulder at any moment, but it doesn't come. And eventually, I slow down to catch my breath and check behind me. And when I do, no one is following me.

I'm alone.

BIRD FACT #20

Cuban trogons often fly in pairs

I've not been to Dunton Mayfield before, but it's nice, I suppose. It's not as big as Brighton, where Mum takes me to get a new pencil case and school bag every August before school starts again. But it does have windows to look into as I walk along the high street.

There are lots of charity shops, with headless

mannequins wearing frilly wedding dresses. There's a bakery, which makes me sigh as I walk past, but I don't stop to get anything. There's a pub and a betting shop and a funeral parlour, which are all shops for adults and not interesting at all. And there's a travel agency, which has a list of holidays on postcards in the window.

I shouldn't really stop, because people might recognize me at any moment, but it would be strange to walk by and not read the holidays in the window. Whenever Mum takes me shopping, we always stop to look at them. She likes to imagine we're jetting off to a deserted island somewhere, where we'll get to lie on the sand and drink from coconuts. If Dad's with us, he'll always point to Greece and Egypt and all the ancient tombs he could explore there. And Rosie always lists the unusual birds in each of the places, like the beautiful Cuban trogon, or the white-tailed hummingbird in Mexico.

I always liked hearing about the different birds, but mainly I enjoyed hearing all about the adventures we could have all together as a family – on beaches and in ancient tombs, too. We could never afford to go to any of those places though.

Seeing my face reflected in the glass makes me step away from the window slightly – I look like a ghost. And my head moves over the head of a picture of another boy, laughing as his dad throws him into a huge swimming pool, with his mum and sister waiting to catch him. Suddenly, I want to shout at the top of my lungs that I am Jasper Wilde – the missing boy from the news – so I can be caught and not have to keep pushing this falling feeling away.

I can feel the eyes of people looking at me strangely – maybe because they recognize me, or because I'm crying a bit. So I put on my sunglasses again and hurry away from the travel agent's.

Eventually, I get out of the main town to a place with car parks and big buildings that sell things to do with DIY and carpets. The people here are walking about on the phone, or are carrying things that look heavy, so they're staring at me less.

I'm really thirsty now though, and I don't think crying helped. I stuff my hands in my pocket and feel the coins, weighing my trousers down. And across the zebra crossing in front of me is a big supermarket with a car park the size of my whole school.

It's important to be prepared when you go on a walk, and not having any food or water isn't being prepared at all. So, looking both ways and using the crossing, I walk through the lines of cars to the main shop entrance, keeping my eyes on my boots.

There's a person at the door smiling at people as they go in, but I avoid their eye and don't look at them. The supermarket is big, with all kinds of things I don't need on my walk and some things I want but don't need, like wildlife magazines. But at the front near the doors is a little kiosk with a fridge of food and drinks, so I quickly scuttle over and choose a bottle of water. I look for one of Mum and Dad's seedy-nut bars to buy too, but they don't have any of those. Dad always complains about other types being our competitors, so instead I pick up a bag of popcorn.

Keeping my head so far down that my chin is almost on my chest, I put the water and the popcorn on the counter to pay. The checkout lady scans them slowly, blowing bubbles with her gum. I don't know if she's looking at me or not, but I can feel myself glowing red-hot.

'One ninety,' she says, in a bored voice.

I quickly throw two pound coins at her and one of them rolls off the counter, so she tuts and has to bend down. And I'm almost thinking about running away now without my change, but I don't know if that's suspicious, so I stand still until she slides ten pence back on a receipt, which I quickly stuff into my pocket and run for the doors.

For a moment, I think maybe I've got away with it and everything. I lift my head up as I run under the giant exit sign. And then I stop still and freeze because there – standing at the entrance doors in neatly pressed uniform – are two police officers.

Flightless birds like emus will often travel great distances on foot or by water to find food

This is it. They've found me and I'm going to be taken away and now I'll never find Rosie.

I forget to look down again, because I'm too busy

staring at the officers' uniforms, my insides flipping over like being on a rollercoaster. They're both dressed all in black and wearing vests with lots of pockets and a belt of things – including probably handcuffs. And out from all of that glimmers a shiny badge and a bright-blue patch saying 'POLICE'.

I close my eyes, put my wrists together and wait for them to be cuffed. I'm sorry sorry sorry, the guilt lying heavy in my stomach. Sorry for not being able to find Rosie and bring her back.

Nothing happens. I squint open an eye and see the officers are still standing at the entrance, speaking to the security guard and an older boy, who also looks like he's feeling guilty about something.

They've not spotted me.

Heart thumping, I'm shaking like a tree in a storm as I tiptoe away from them. I daren't look up in case they see me, so try my hardest to look natural and like I'm not the missing boy they're looking for. I join in at the edge of a family walking to their car, laughing at the joke one of the dads said like I belong to them, so the man looks at me, strangely.

My thoughts are wild and I feel the panic in my chest like a kettle bubbling up. I run out of the car park, down the road, checking behind me for blue lights and hearing sirens in my ears.

I haven't got my map in my hands and my eyes are blurry. I take a wrong turn down a road with old shopping trolleys in it, and then circle around the back of a warehouse. And everything around me looks lost and suddenly I feel lost, too.

'Rosie?' I say, out loud.

But she's not here to help me. And I think back to the news article with my face on and that word dives in my head again with its great talons out.

'Tragically . . .'

I won't listen to it and I can't. My breathing is getting funny again, so I practise Gan's rules for panic attacks and count until my thoughts turn back to facts.

Rosie is my sister and she's always there for me, no matter what. Things go away, but they come back again – just like birds on their migration. Just like lost dogs and bird tags and footballs.

Things aren't lost. They're only ever in a different place. And I'm walking to that place with everything I have and I'm going to find the nightingale.

Gan's hurt face when he found his broken football

swims in my mind and I close my eyes tight, thinking of bird facts.

FACTS ABOUT MIGRATION

Some larger birds like geese follow older relatives on their migration, but many smaller birds take their first trips alone. It's thought that birds are born with an internal compass, showing them the way.

Calmer now, I take out my map again. Pull my hat as far down on my head as I can.

And I find my way back to the path.

Some birds travel over sixteen thousand miles on their migration

I walk into some long, winding streets past houses that all look the same. There are people out on their driveways washing cars and mowing lawns. My watch says it's 4 p.m. now, and I wonder what Mum and Dad

are up to and how
worried about me they are
now. I hope they're not feeling too
bad, as they've been worried a lot this
week and I really don't want to make it worse.
I can't let them find me, though. Not yet.

A tree-lined alleyway has a sign saying 'The Great
Oak Trail'. This is marked with big green spots on my
map, which means it's a proper walking route for hikers.
The route stretches all the way to Rosie's university and
we've done bits of it before, so I know that it's got lots of
signposts and will be easier to follow than the scraggly
footpaths around fields and farms.

As I get further away from the houses, the trees seem to sprout up more and more, and soon, I'm walking in a forest. The ground is squelchy and feels like a trampoline, and there are paths forking off in every direction. If Rosie were walking with me, I know she'd want to walk every single one. I'm careful to stick to the main route though, squinting in the dark of the trees and strange, birdless silence.

I usually like forests, but this one reminds me of my dream last night. I can't see any people, but I can hear rustling in the bushes around me and feel eyes watching me. Thorns reach their fingers out and grab at my ankles, and spiders spin webs to catch me in. I walk faster and faster until I'm running, checking the map again and again as I leap over gooey puddles and snap twigs under my boots.

Eventually, I can't run any more so I stop, my hands on my knees, panting. A honey bee is wriggling on the edge of a puddle in front of me. Bending down, it looks like it's got wet and is struggling to get away from the water, which must feel like a black angry sea to such a small thing. I try to fish it out with a stick, but I'm worried about hurting its tiny wings, so instead I dip my index finger into the puddle and gently push it to safety.

The bee buzzes and flaps and I feel like I've made a difference to him. I'm just telling him that everything will be fine – like Gan did to me when I was panicking – when I feel a sharp pain stab into the top of my finger.

My cry finds the hiding birds in the trees and sends them flapping into the sky away from me. There's a black sting in my finger and it throbs with pain now, making the tears come again, because I thought I was doing something good, when I wasn't. And now everything is going wrong and I feel it inside my heart like the bee stung that too.

'Oh now, what's all this?' a voice says softly from behind me.

I spin round and fall over, so my non-stung hand gets covered in mud. There – standing tall above me – is the oldest man I've ever seen, wearing a woolly hat and the same jumper as me, but in a bigger size.

The old man crouches down with me on the floor, looking at my stung finger.

'Tush, tush, tush,' he says, quietly, putting on a pair of wide glasses that he had hooked into the neck of his jumper. 'May I?'

I nod and hold my finger out to him and his skin feels papery. He uses a ridged thumbnail to push the sting out from my finger, making me suck in my breath.

'That's it, nice and brave.'

I don't feel brave. I feel tired and stung and alone. But the man takes off the big bag he had on his back, which is the same kind of bag the man on the front of one of the seedy-nut bars is wearing when he's on top of a mountain, and he takes out a tube of sting cream, dabbing a little on the end of my finger.

'Is that better?'

I nod, sniffing.

At school, the teachers are always saying that it's important not to talk to strangers. But I don't think I've been doing a good job of listening to that so far, because I spoke to Lulu, Madge and Gan. But all of those were nice people, so I guess I was lucky.

And I think I'm lucky again with this old man, as he shuffles over to the sad-looking bee in the puddle and starts singing to it in another language.

He lifts it carefully onto his own finger and his song sounds sad and beautiful. And then he stops and says, 'His soul bird has flown away,' and lays it carefully in the grass to the side of the path, so it doesn't get accidentally trodden on.

It's exactly what Rosie would do if she were here.

Apart from the 'soul bird' thing, because I don't know what they are, and they aren't in my book. But Rosie was stung by a bee too once. It was hiding in her Coke can and when she took a swig of it, it stung her on the lip.

Rosie doesn't cry that often, because she says there isn't really any need to. But that day, she cried for hours and hours.

Mum said, 'It can't hurt that much, Ro!'

But Rosie shook her head and said, 'I'm not crying for me. I'm crying for the bee.'

That's when I learned that bees usually die when they sting people. And however much Rosie believes that dying is just a part of living, she hates it when animals die because of something stupid that humans do – like dropping litter, or driving too fast in their car, or drinking from a Coke can.

So we had a funeral for the bee in the garden, and buried it in a matchbox. We all said some nice words about him, and how we hoped there were a lot of sugary drinks wherever he was buzzing off to. And Rosie seemed to cheer up at that, because we had buried it, and its body was part of the circle of life again, helping to feed lots of other animals.

'I was only trying to help it,' I say, quietly.

The old man crouches back with me on the ground, looking up into the tops of the trees overhead like they are whispering things to him. 'Not everything is good at knowing when to accept help.'

He turns then and looks at me, and I feel his tree-brown eyes staring into me like he knows all my secrets, and I quickly try to hide my face again under my hat.

'You're part of the Dunton Mayfield Junior Ramblers?' he asks, pointing at the badge on the jumper I'm wearing. 'I don't recognize you, but then we've had so many new children join recently!' He smiles, brightly. 'Are you one of the new ones?'

I don't really want to lie to him, but also I'm worried that he might know who I am, so I quickly nod and hope I'm not going too red.

He taps the badge on his own jumper, which is the same.

'You're not a junior though,' I say.

The old man looks surprised for a moment and says, 'What do you mean? I'm ten years old!'

And I look at his wrinkled face and gappy grin with my own mouth wide open before he laughs out loud. 'Ha ha! No. I am eighty years young. But someone has got to make sure all you young ramblers are keeping in check, don't they?' His eyes twinkle. 'I volunteered to go at the back today, to make sure no one is left behind on our Great Oak Trail ramble to Horton's Cross.'

He stands up and offers his hand to help me up. I'm not sure what to do. The old man thinks I'm on a group walk with the Dunton Mayfield Junior Ramblers. I should correct him and tell him that I'm on my own and on a whole different walk to find my sister. But also, he's found me, now, and I'm not sure what will happen if he knows the truth.

'Do you have a mobile phone . . . ?' I ask, slowly.

The old man laughs and shakes his head so hard that his hat slips over his eyebrows. 'Did you not hear, I'm eighty years old! Who do you think I'm going to text message?'

I smile and grab his hand, so he pulls me all the way up.

'I'm Jasper,' I say, keeping my hand in his to shake it.

'Ibrahim,' the old man says.

We let go and put our bags back on, looking out at the footpath ahead of us. 'Okay, Jasper. Are you okay if I walk you back to your group?'

And I think about my group and what that really

means. Rosie and the nightingale. Maybe also Mum, Dad, Fish the cat and even my granny. I nod.

I remember Horton's Cross on my map. It's the place where Ibrahim's walk ends, and I leave the Great Oak Trail for the last tiny bit of walk to the motorway services. And even though I'm not sure if I should be walking with an old man, or if getting away from him later will be difficult, I'm also pleased to have the forest turn back into a nice place again, with him walking by my side.

There are more chickens on earth than there are people

I thought that Ibrahim might slow me down, but he isn't slow at all. If anything, he's almost too fast, and I keep having to pretend to do up my shoelaces so I can catch my breath.

My granny is seventy-five and she can hardly walk at all. She likes to play chess and watch TV, but can't walk a long way because of her bad hips. I thought that was what all old people were like.

'How come you're so good at walking?'

He laughs. 'A man is as wise as his head, not his years.'

I shake my head. 'What does that mean?'

He takes big huge strides and throws his arms around like the whole field belongs to him. 'It's a proverb. In my home country, my father always tried to keep me in line with proverbs.' His eyes twinkle mischieviously again. 'That one means that you're as young as you think, and I think young.'

I smile, because although Ibrahim looks old, his smile does remind me of Gan a little bit.

'It also means that just because I'm old, it doesn't mean I'm wise.' He laughs a lot at that again.

'You seem wise to me. You knew what to do with my bee sting and it feels much better now.'

Ibrahim makes his face mock-serious. 'Oh yes, I'm very responsible.' But then he starts laughing again, so I'm not sure he really believes that's true.

As we walk, I notice his hand keeps going to the

front pocket of his shirt. He'll tap it twice, or whisper something to it in another language. And when I peer over, I can see something that looks like a piece of paper hiding in it.

And it makes me wonder if Ibrahim is the same as Lulu, Madge and Gan.

'Ibrahim, what is it that you've lost?' I ask.

He opens a gate for me and I step through. 'What do you mean, lost?'

'Well, everyone else I've met on my walk so far has lost something and I've helped them find it. So I could help you too, if you like.'

'Is that why you were walking so far at the back?' I hide my face as he closes the gate again, forgetting that I was supposed to be on the walk he thinks I am. But he shakes his head. 'I have everything I need.' He pats his front shirt pocket again. 'Not lost at all.'

We walk past a row of houses and some chickens pecking at the side of the road, pretending they are wild and free, and I keep my head hidden, in case anyone is looking out of their windows for me.

'But there must be something,' I say.

We get to another gate with a huge puddle on the other side. Ibrahim hops over it with his long legs and I

160

sit on the top looking at the water. I'm not very good at long jumping, even with a run-up, and this puddle is big and looks deep.

'Maybe it's time for you to stop stopping to help others,' he says, picking up a broken brick from the bush. 'Maybe it's time to let someone else help you. Like your bee should have done.'

He throws the brick into the puddle and muddy water sploshes out and down like a fountain, before swirling and glugging bubbles around the brand-new stepping stone he made for me.

'A good companion shortens the longest road.'

He holds out his hand to me. It would be easy now to hop onto the brick and across to the other side.

Getting to Rosie is the one thing I've wanted to do as quick as I can for this whole walk. But now I'm so close, I suddenly feel like maybe I don't want my long journey to get any shorter.

Ibrahim smiles and nods to the brick. But I don't need his help. I don't need friends at school, or parents to listen to me, to be able to jump over a puddle, or find my missing sister.

I'll do it. I'll just do it in my own time.

Thinking about it for a while, I imagine myself

jumping like a widowbird. Widowbirds are found in Kenya and Tanzania and have really long tails they like to show off in jumping competitions to attract attention in the long grass. I imagine myself with long tail feathers, grit my teeth and kick off from the gate, pushing myself high and far. Ibrahim's mouth opens wide as he watches me land the other side of the puddle with a squelch. And he claps his hands together as I try to hide my face, because I can feel water in my shoe from where I didn't quite make it all the way, and I have mud all over my hand from where I slipped when I landed.

But I made it. All by myself.

Ibrahim dances off in front of me and I follow him in my soggy socks. I know that he's lost something, even if he won't tell me what it is. And I know that I'm brave enough to find anything. Even a missing sister.

Even if it takes for ever.

Winter roosts of starlings can hold millions of birds

We walk along a path that's had its middle scooped out. We have to put one foot in the bottom and one at the top on the edge to go along it, so walking feels more like wobbling. And even though I'm still worrying about how close we are now and how it's almost dinner time already, I can hear sounds of larks and tits, and the

starling

breeze shaking trees like tissue paper, which calms me down.

The sky looks like a big blue lake with planes floating in it. Some of the planes ripple the sky into froth and leave trails of white bubbles for the birds to have a bath in.

I think the birds are enjoying the fact the rain from yesterday has gone, because they're not hiding any more, but racing loop-the-loops and diving deep into the blue.

I keep my eye on them and try to guess out loud what I think they are, which is difficult to do when the birds are in the sky and not singing from the trees.

But then I hear something and stop dead mid-wobble.

'Jasper—'

'Shhh,' I say. 'Listen.'

We listen and it sounds like a magpie. But then the sound topples into a sparrow call, and then what sounds like someone sawing through a whole forest of trees and hammering some nails into a bit of wood, and then I realize that it's a starling.

It's a bit like listening to people who can beatbox. Ms Li showed us a video of beatboxers in music class last term, because it involved making sounds with only our mouths and our bodies. Some of the people on the video sounded like they had entire bands with drum kits and bass guitars and whistles hidden between their lips.

Starlings are the most brilliant beatboxers though, better than any human, probably.

'Is that all one bird?' Ibrahim says, his eyes closed and his face pointed to the sky.

'Just one,' I say. 'Starlings can mimic things. They can learn the songs of all kinds of other birds, and the sounds of things they probably shouldn't learn too, like car alarms. It's strange hearing a bird be a car alarm, but other than that it's good, isn't it?'

Ibrahim nods, his eyes still closed, and I smile because he is listening.

'Only the nightingale is better at singing. They know hundreds of different songs. Have you ever heard one?'

Ibrahim shakes his head. And then he starts singing himself.

His song starts quiet at first, but then gets louder. I look around to see if anyone is watching, but it's just us on the path for as far as I can see. The starling stops, and all the other birds seem to as well, so I close my eyes like him and I listen.

The song is in another language, but I think it must be about being on a train – there's a *chug chug chug*, and long notes as we seem to go through tunnels. There's a sad part, but then there's hope joined up into it and it makes me see Rosie's face, listening somewhere to the nightingale under another tree, with her face up to the sky like ours are. And it feels like we're listening to the same song even though we're squares away, together and apart, all at once.

Ibrahim stops singing and there are minutes where the whole world seems to be stuck for words.

'What language is that?'

He opens his eyes and blinks around like he's just noticed where we are. 'Turkish. It was my first language, before I moved here with my wife – sixty years ago now.'

'It's beautiful,' I say. 'Are you a professional singer?'

'I was once. My wife and I were in a band. We walked the whole country singing to people, at weddings, and festivals and even just on the streets. Whenever someone was there to listen, we would sing.' Ibrahim taps his heart pocket again, his eyes far away.

'Where's your wife now? Is she part of the Dunton Mayfield Junior Ramblers, too?'

His face cracks slightly and my stomach jumps and I wish the question back through my lips, like I could suck it back up through a straw.

'She was, once,' he says, resting his hand on his pocket now. 'But now, she's in a better place.'

The words charge through my whole body like an electric shock and I jolt backwards, so Ibrahim jumps and looks around for what hurt me.

It was him. Those words swarm like bees with dagger stings, along with that other word too . . .

'Tragically.'

I can't listen. Can't think.

So I put my hands over my ears and run.

The nightingale is part of a family of birds called 'chats'

I always thought words were brilliant, true things that could help calm me down. But Ibrahim's face when he said that his wife was in the Better Place mixes with my dad's when he said it to me and now the words are like thorns.

'Rosie has gone to a Better Place,' Dad said.

That means she's with our nightingale. She's up a tree, listening to the song in the ink-dusk, waiting for me to join her and feel like everything in the world is right again.

I don't want to know what Ibrahim has lost any more.

I run and run down the narrow path, stumbling on the uneven ground. My eyes are blurry, my head full of panic, so I don't see the rabbit hole burrowed into the path.

'Ouch!' I shout, my ankle twisting as I crumble to the ground clutching my foot.

The pain mixes in with all the other bad things and I sit with my bum on the ground and start crying.

There's a shuffle as Ibrahim bends down to me. I want to tell him to go away and leave me alone, but I also don't want that at all. He looks at my ankle and twists it gently left and right, looking at me the whole time but not saying anything.

'Your ankle is okay, I think,' he says with a kind smile. 'It was just a sprain – you're lucky.'

I don't feel lucky. Ibrahim hands me a tissue and watches me carefully as I wipe my eyes, looking left and right up the path.

'Do *you* have a mobile phone, Jasper?'

I shake my head. 'It's broken.'

Ibrahim looks worried now. I should feel worried about that too, but I just feel tired and confused and like I just want to lie down and go to sleep for a bit.

'We should keep moving, it'll be dark soon,' Ibrahim says, looking at the sky that is still bright blue, but that my watch says will be ink-black in just two hours.

'I don't want to,' I say, in a small voice.

I can tell Ibrahim isn't sure, but he nods and sits down with me, even though it's really muddy and his trousers are light coloured, like mine.

'Okay,' he says. 'It's teatime, anyway.'

My stomach grumbles as he opens his big bag and pulls out an entire picnic. He's brought all kinds of things – sandwiches, tea cakes, olives, chocolate bars and cherries, which are wrapped up in kitchen roll from where they have been washed in the sink. I just pick at the fruit first, but then I start to feel better, so I eat three sandwiches, a tea cake and a handful of olives, too. It's all quite sweet and salty, so I drink most of the bottle of water he gives me in one go.

'I'm sorry for running away.'

He nods at me. 'Did you want to tell me why? You are safe with me, Jasper.'

171

I do feel safe with Ibrahim. And it's strange, because just a few days ago I would have thought it impossible that I could feel that way about a grown-up I don't know – let alone have whole conversations with him. But telling anyone what I'm thinking right now feels like it might free the eagle of panic that I'm keeping caged up in my chest and I'm scared.

Instead, I point out the birds I hear in the trees, like a robin alarming a warning call, and a blackcap and a real house sparrow, not a pretend starling one. With each one I find, I feel a little less panicky and a little stronger.

'Very good, very good,' Ibrahim says, looking quite impressed.

'My big sister Rosie taught me a lot of them,' I say, keeping my eyes on my boots. 'It all started with the nightingale. She'd sneak me out of the house when she was supposed to be getting me ready for bed when I was little, and she'd help me climb up our tree. Then we'd just sit there waiting for it and it was like everything.'

'Everything,' Ibrahim whispers. 'I like that.'

'Then when I got older, we'd go for walks too, and she told me that birdsong is like a big complicated puzzle, because birds talk over each other all at once and the pieces get jumbled. But once you know what all those pieces sound like, then it's easier to take them out and start un-puzzling it.'

I look at Ibrahim out of the sides of my eyes, because I'm expecting him to look bored or angry at me for talking about birds, like Dad sometimes is. But he's listening to me and it feels nice. Maybe this is how Gan felt, when he opened up to me about his dad moving away. Like he could do it because I'd understand.

I lick the salt from my lips. 'The nightingale has come to the field behind our garden every single year since for ever, Ibrahim. But I've been waiting every night this spring so far, and it still hasn't arrived. I know that the numbers of the nightingales are dropping because people keep cutting down the bushes they make their nests in, but I thought our nightingale would be safe because it's near to our house and we always look out for it.' My hands are shaking. 'And it's the same with Rosie, too. I thought . . . I thought she would be safe.'

I can feel Ibrahim looking hard at me.

'When you love someone, you do whatever you can do to find them, don't you?' I ask him.

I wait for Ibrahim to nod or say one of his proverbs, but he doesn't. He sits very still. I wish that he'd stop listening now and tell me that everything is going to be okay – that the nightingale is going to come back. That I'll find Rosie soon and she'll know what to do to make things like they used to be, where a boy and his sister can sit in a tree together.

Eventually, he turns to me and his eyes are sad. 'He that conceals his grief will find no remedy for it. The bravest thing anyone can ever do is speak their truth, Jasper.'

He starts packing the food away and singing again. It's the same song as before, but this time, the train sounds like it may be falling off the tracks.

BIRD FACT #26

All mute swans in England and Wales are technically owned by the Queen

Ibrahim and I walk the rest of the path in silence. He wants to walk fast again, but I'm tired and drag my feet. Eventually though, we come out in a park with a climbing frame, swing set and a slide.

The sign says:

WELCOME TO HORTON'S CROSS

There's a teenage girl pushing a boy about my age on the swing. He's going so high, it's like he'll go all the way around and over the top, but he's still calling for her to push him higher and higher. And the girl pushes and laughs and her cheeks are bright red.

The girl doesn't look like Rosie. And the boy doesn't look like me, because going that high on a swing frightens me. But it still makes my bones twang.

Ahead of us is the river I remember seeing on the map like a fat snake, slithering between oak trees and rocks. I need to cross the river and walk into another field after that, but Ibrahim's walk finishes here.

Ibrahim looks around for the other people in his group, but I can't see anyone else wearing green sweaters. 'We should find help now,' he says, quietly.

My panic is clogging in my throat, because I don't know what to do. I want Ibrahim to keep walking with me to find Rosie, but I don't think he will, and I can't tell him that I've been lying to him.

He starts along the path into the town, when suddenly we hear a call.

'Help! Help us!'

Ibrahim spins round, arms out like he's a superhero ready to take off and fly into action. We look around and see two younger boys who look like the same person copy-and-pasted, jumping and waving their hats at us from the riverbank.

Even though they sound afraid, their calls make relief flood through my whole body.

Ibrahim jogs towards them and I follow. 'Are you okay?' he asks.

The boys are both out of breath from the jumping they've been doing. They are identical and it isn't helping that they're dressed in the same dungarees, with the same spiky hair.

'It's our dad,' the boy on the left says.

'His boat has got stuck, and now he's lost way over there,' the boy on our right says.

We look out across the water, which is chattering

over mossy rocks and green reeds. And close to the bank on the other side is an embarrassed-looking man in a rowing boat, stuck on a swan's nest.

'It's okay, honestly,' their dad shouts across to us. 'I can probably just . . .'

He rocks the boat side to side and his arms fly up as it tips, nearly plunging him in.

Ibrahim looks at me. 'I don't think . . .'

But the twin closest to me looks afraid. 'Please,' he says. 'He's been stuck for ages, and we don't know what to do.'

The other twin picks up an oar lying on the grass. 'He dropped both of these. We managed to get one, but the other has been lost.'

'We need to find help ourselves,' Ibrahim says, looking like a proper grown-up now and not a boy in an old man's body. 'Does your dad have a mobile phone?'

The twins chatter excitedly to Ibrahim and the river has jumped up into my veins and I can feel its spluttery panic. I'm going to get caught and arrested by the police if I don't get away right now.

So, like I've been doing all throughout this walk, I push down my panic. I take off my boots, stuff my map in my pocket and pick up the dropped oar. And I take a running jump at the river.

The twins shout out as I fly over the water. 'He's doing it!'

I land on a rock spiking up out of the water. It's cold and slippery under my feet and I wobble.

Ibrahim tries to reach out and pull me back. 'Jasper, no! The man can get out the other side – we need to find the others.'

'I'm okay!' I say, steadying myself. 'Look – this happened to Rosie and me once too, when we were in a lake trying to find swans. I dropped the oar into the water, and Rosie showed me a stroke you can do with just one paddle, that will keep you going forwards. You don't even need two for that.' I hold up the oar in my hand. 'Just this one.'

'We need to get you home now, Jasper.'

He sounds worried, but I ignore him. I dig the oar into a muddy patch in front of me, where the water isn't as deep. Then push down on it as I jump, to go further. Then I hop fast – left-right, left-right – across smaller rocks to get to a big one in the middle, which isn't easy to land on, because it's spiky, like a shrunken mountain.

'Be careful!' the man calls from the boat ahead.

I wipe my hand over my face and sort of sit on the

rock for a moment, so I can get my breath back. I've already come almost all the way across the river, and I can see the twins jumping on the bank behind me.

But where is Ibrahim?

Spinning round, I see him running along the riverbank in the wrong direction. He has my boots, so I call out to him to tell him to stop. But then he turns to a part of the bank that juts into the river, using his long legs to jump onto the other side.

I stand up quickly and get ready to jump, before Ibrahim beats me to it. The boat is just one tricky rock away from me now. I expect to see the man in it looking impressed at how a panicky boy can make it all the way over a river to save him when he couldn't do it himself, but instead he is staring. At me.

I wobble again.

'Aren't you that missing boy from the news?' he asks.

I leap across the final rock and clatter into the boat with my face away from him. 'No. I'm not missing – I'm right here.'

I wedge the oar into the nest and push with all my might, trying to move us, as the man gets his phone out.

The oar drops.

'You look a lot like him. It's all over the news. A boy

ran away from home looking for his sister yesterday and his parents are going nuts, apparently.'

My chest starts to squeeze. And then Ibrahim runs up next to us and puts out his hand from the other bank.

'Jasper,' he says. 'Come.'

But everything is going blurry because I've been found.

The man digs the oar hard into the nest. 'Good job you've got your grandad with you,' he says, cheerfully. 'That missing kid from the news is all alone, poor chap. And with what happened to his sister too . . . Tragic thing.'

My blood feels hot.

I want to ask.

What is the tragic thing? What?

But I also want to push him away and break the phone and not ask a question like that ever. I look at Ibrahim to try to stop him from listening too, because the words are making the river whip into an angry sea.

'Missing kid from the news?' he asks slowly.

The man hands Ibrahim his phone and Ibrahim looks.

And I scramble to the side of the boat and stretch and try to snatch the phone away.

But then Ibrahim reads something. Something awful. I can tell by the way the light disappears and his eyes get dead-crow dark.

He looks at me, and his face cracks.
It feels like I have fallen.
Dropped.
Right into the freezing water.

Only the hummingbird can fly backwards

I jump.

With everything, I jump.

I don't fall into the water and Rosie is fine fine fine. I'm going to find her. Right now, at the motorway services, where she'll be listening to our nightingale – in her Better Place.

I jump.

Onto the riverbank and away from the man and his stuck boat, because it's stupid for me to keep stopping when I should have been walking all this time and I'm sorry, Rosie.

'Jasper,' Ibrahim says. Clutching my boots.

But I don't need him. I don't need anyone or anything. I am all Rosie needs and she's all I need, too.

So I run again.

I can hear the twins crying, because I didn't save their dad. But he said something about a tragic thing, so he can just stay stuck for all I care.

I can also hear Ibrahim running behind me, trying to get me to stop. But he's very old and I'm not going to stop. I'm not going to stop again until I've found Rosie and told her that I'm sorry for taking so long.

'I didn't know,' he keeps saying, over and over. 'Your jumper, I thought . . .'

'There's nothing to know!' I shout over the thundering water. Ibrahim's face is full of worry, lines and wide eyes staring.

The twigs and rocks hiding under the grass spike into my feet and the air stitches between my ribs.

The gate that will take me back into the wilderness, to the motorway services, is there. I turn and snatch my boots from a panting Ibrahim and stamp them on without my socks. I start to climb over the stile, but he stops me with a hand on my shoulder.

'Jasper, you need help . . .'

I throw Ibrahim off me and he takes a step back because I'm made of fire and it hurts, hurts, hurts.

'I don't need ANYTHING!' I roar, so loud that the crows hiding in the trees burst out and clap their wings together. 'I'm brave and I'm clever. I walked a long way by myself before I even met you and I don't need you! Just go home.'

He raises his hands, looking afraid, and he should be. 'Your parents are very worried. I need to take you home now, Jasper. You need to slow down.'

His words charge like lightning down through my bones and into my legs and I kick them into the gate, over and over, not stopping though it hurts my toe. I can't. It makes a horrible clanging sound that sends the birds shrieking from the trees, but at least that's drowning out the bad things in my head. I need that word I heard to get out of my brain. But Ibrahim read it. And I saw his eyes when he did.

'Go away!' I turn and shout at him, clenching my fists. 'You're just a stupid old man who acts like a little boy and I don't want you here!'

He looks sad. 'A knife-wound heals, but a tongue-wound festers.'

That just makes me madder. But I can't scream anything else because my words have all gone, so I just climb over the gate. Ibrahim catches the handles on the top of my bag, but I wriggle out of it and run away, so he's left holding it on the other side of the gate.

The grass on the other side is long, and although Ibrahim is fast, he's not as small and as good at hiding as me. I run faster than I ever have.

'Jasper!' Ibrahim calls over and over. 'Jasper, please!'

I jump over a small creek, push myself down a bank on the other side so I'm sliding, sliding until at the bottom I can hide myself in the middle of the long grass. Plastering my hand over my mouth to stop me breathing so fast, I stay as still as I can, even though I can feel the cold, wet mud seeping into my clothes.

Ibrahim is above, still shouting my name. So I tell him with my inside voice to leave me alone. To take those words he read away with him, because they're not welcome at all. But as I hear his calls get fainter and fainter, the world seems to get darker.

Heron

BIRD FACT #28

Herons can have wings two times the size of their body

Lying in the mud, I think I'm crying, but I'm a bit too cold to really know.

My head is full of Rosie.

I'm thinking about my birthday, when I turned nine years old. I want to read about it in our *Book of Birds*, but it's in my bag with Ibrahim. And even though my chest is fizzing with panic like a whole multipack of pierced Coke cans, I can't calm it down with any other story.

Mum and Dad told me that turning nine was going to be my best birthday yet, because it was my last birthday in single digits before I turned ten. But Mum and Dad are bad at keeping promises these days and this birthday was just the same. They locked themselves away and promised to come out, but they never did. So I called Rosie.

She drove back straight away and took me to the reservoir, which is this huge lake that stretches so far, it almost looks like the ocean.

'Were we supposed to bring swimming trunks? Because I didn't,' I said as we got out of her rusty car.

'You'll have to go in your pants then,' she said, nudging me, but it was just a joke, because there were lots of signs around saying that you weren't allowed to swim. So we started walking around the outside of the water.

On our walk, we saw a massive heron take off in the

sky, looking like a dragon. We saw a gaggle of geese, honking over each other. And there were mallards and egrets, and other non-water birds too, like swifts and wagtails and treecreepers. I counted them all out loud, so I'd remember to put them in our *Book of Birds* later.

Then I saw a shape far out in the water and I thought it might be an otter, because it looked like it had fur. I stopped and grabbed Rosie, because otters are rare to see.

I looked through my binoculars and stared at it flapping around in the middle of the water.

'It kind of looks like a cat.'

'Give them here,' Rosie said, snatching the binoculars off me, but keeping them around my neck, so I choked a bit. She ignored my complaining and focused on the thing in the water.

'It's a kitten,' she said.

My back prickled. 'But kittens don't swim, do they?'

Rosie didn't answer. She took off her shoes and coat and gave me her phone and her car keys out of her pocket. And then she started walking into the water.

'Rosie!' I hissed. 'You can't go in in your clothes!'

'It's okay,' she said, still walking. 'I've done it before.' The water was up to her chest now and I could tell it was cold because she was gasping. 'I'll be careful, don't worry.'

And then she started swimming. And at the bank it was silent, but inside my head was a rock band, drumming drumming drumming. I looked around for something to save her with if she needed it, but there wasn't a rubber ring or anything. It was just me all alone and I'm not very good at swimming.

She swam up to the thing she said was a kitten, and there was some splashing for a moment, before she started floating. I grabbed the binoculars again. The view was shaky in my hands, but I saw Rosie on her back, clutching a tiny ball of black fur on her chest.

She started to paddle herself backwards, and it took a long time. I was worried about hypothermia and drowning and whether there was anything in the water that might eat her, because the signs said not to swim and there must be a reason for that.

When she got close enough, she picked the cat up and turned to walk out of the water, and it took everything I had not to run in and help her.

She was shivering so much, so I put my coat around her. But she took it straight back off and put it around the cat instead.

'It's just a baby,' she said, all gaspy. 'Still a kitten.'

But I was looking at my sister turning blue and

suddenly I was angry. 'You could have died!' I shouted.

She flicked her eyes up to me and then back down to the kitten, who was looking wet and shocked.

'I was never going to die, silly,' she said.

But I was shaking like I had been in the cold water with her, because I realized that I was thinking it for the whole five minutes she was saving the cat, and it felt horrible.

'It's my birthday!' I shouted. 'Imagine if you had died on my birthday!'

She took my hand and hers felt like ice.

'I would never do that to you,' she said. 'But if I hadn't gone in, this kitten would have died. And that wouldn't have helped anything.'

She looked at me and smiled at me and shivered. And I believed her. I believed that she wouldn't ever do that to me, because Rosie is always there. Even when Mum and Dad aren't, she is.

And I thought that was a solid, unchangeable fact.

Kestrel

Birds like kestrels can often be seen hovering over motorway verges

Head down, my feet keep going, one in front of the other.

I think about Fish the cat at home and wonder if she's been okay since I left her yesterday. When Rosie saved her in the reservoir, the vet said she was lucky to have survived and that was all down to Rosie. We got to take her home with us the next day, but Mum didn't want to keep her because she was annoyed at Rosie for taking such a risk.

'Well, maybe if you were there for Jasper's birthday like you promised, then I wouldn't have had to drive him to the reservoir in the first place!' Rosie shouted at her.

Mum looked like she was going to say something else, but then she saw that I was there and lowered her voice. 'Rosie, you know it's not as easy as that. The business is finally making money, if we stop now—'

Rosie picked up Fish the cat and gave her to me. 'Here, Jasper,' she said. 'Look after Fish for me. Show Mum what being there for something really means.'

And I promised that I would, but in a quiet voice. Because Rosie's shouts seemed to have stopped Mum from working. She just sat there and looked at me for hours and hours. And then she stood up and drove me to town to buy bags of food and litter and toys.

Taking the map out of my pocket I see that it's only one square to the motorway services now. I join up with a long tarmacked path that people are cycling on, and

I keep my face hidden under my hat. I walk through tunnels under roads where the cars above have started to turn their lights on, ready for the night.

It's starting to get to that time now. It's eight o'clock, and the sun will be all-the-way down soon.

My throat still hurts from when I shouted at Ibrahim, and when I think about how the lines on his face started dipping down, it makes me twist up on the inside.

He's probably found someone with a phone now and called the police. I'm not mad about that, because I would probably call the police on someone who said such nasty things to me, too. But it does mean I have to hurry faster than ever now if I'm ever going to find Rosie before they catch me.

As I rush along the path, it gets darker and darker. I stop seeing people around me walking dogs and riding bikes. I stop being able to see into the distance and it feels like the world is closing around me. It's scary, walking alone in a place I don't know in the dark, and some of me wishes that Ibrahim would just appear suddenly and walk the rest of the way by my side. Instead, I try to think of some bird facts.

FACTS ABOUT BIRDS AT SUNSET

Some birds like rooks and crows can flock together at sunset in spectacular numbers before they settle down to roost for the night. Starling murmurations can look like twirling ribbons in the sky, made out of thousands of birds all flying together.

I can't see any flocks or murmurations of birds, but soon, through the darkness, I hear the roaring of traffic, like putting a shell over your ear to hear the sea. Only this is a sea of exhaust pipes and rattling lorries and motorbikes.

The motorway is a thick blue snake on my map, but in real life it's like a line of yellow fire.

Cars rocket up and down it so fast that they're just blurs. There aren't any street lights on the road – just the lights from the front and back of the cars, which makes the road flicker yellow and red like flames.

starling

I have to cross it. But not on the road, because motorways aren't for walking on. Even if your car breaks down on a motorway, you have to pull over and get out because it's so dangerous.

Luckily for me, there's a bridge. It's wide enough for a car to be on, but there aren't any around. I walk to the side anyway, and look over the top of the bridge to the cars under me, speeding by like deafening whispers.

On the other side of the bridge, there is a row of trees, and I follow the road around until it spits me out at a roundabout. There on the other side, lit up in bright lights, is the place that I've walked all this way to get to.

The motorway services.

I'm so happy to see it that I call out and almost fall over, because I'm tired and sore. They are there, somewhere. Rosie and the nightingale. They just have to be.

The roundabout is huge with dented barriers in the middle. There are four exits, and each one is filled up with cars with bright brake lights and flashing indicators. I look for the pedestrian crossing, and find the little bumps on the ground that say I can cross, but no green man to help me.

I count that I need to cross two roads. So I stand and wait for the traffic lights to turn red for the cars, and a big lorry goes by and pushes me with so much wind that I almost fall over again. But I steady myself. And I wait and I wait again. Then I'm getting nervous because all this waiting is stopping me from seeing Rosie, but I have to stay safe because I promised Mum and Dad that I would.

Then I see the red light and the cars all roll to a stop. I dash quickly across the road, even though I know you shouldn't because you could trip and fall. Making it to the other side, I jump over the metal barrier and get oil on my hands before jogging across the verge to the next barrier.

This road is harder to cross, because the cars aren't coming in a line, they're coming off the roundabout in all kinds of directions. I wait for the red light again, but then spot what I think is a gap and lean forward to run, and a motorbike comes out of nowhere and nearly knocks me over.

My blood feels hot and I want to sit down, but there's no time. So as soon as I see the red light, I just take it at a run, crossing the white lines in the middle and—

I make it.

The other side of the barriers from the cars is a big petrol station, where lorries are filling up from huge tanks hidden under the ground. I walk fast down the road, seeing buildings with symbols outside for toilets and cafes and restaurants that sell chips. And I put my hands in my pockets and feel the money that I was saving to buy some for Rosie and I promise her in my head that I'll buy some as soon as I see where she is.

There's a huge car park with a lot of cars in it, but I can't see Rosie's purple one in the dark. There are people walking with their hands in their pockets. There are street lamps and bins and parked caravans.

And I can't imagine why a nightingale would ever choose to live here and not in our nice field back home. But then I notice a thicket of trees down the very back of the car park, where less people are because it means further to walk. If I were a nightingale, I'm sure that I would choose to go there if I found myself lost at a service station.

I'm speeding up now, half running across the car park, arms tight at my sides, my fists and teeth clenched. I can hear the roar of the motorway still from across the way, and a car alarm somewhere, but no birds. It's night now and a lot of birds go to sleep at this time.

I dodge a parked car and another one that's moving, and I walk towards the trees. Listening.

'Please be here, please be here, please.'

I step up from the tarmac. And as soon as my foot hits the grass, I hear it.

A nightingale song is one of the most beautiful sounds on the planet

The nightingale sings.

It sings and then it stops. Then it sings a different song, then it stops again.

The song is so loud, I feel it vibrating in my ear. It

blasts into the black night sky and makes the new stars twinkle.

It's the sound my heart makes and what my bones sing back. And if you cut me open, you'd find little brown feathers and a chest full of notes I haven't even sung yet.

I stand with my feet on the grass, like I am planted, looking up to the night and I listen listen listen.

If I close my eyes, it almost feels like I am home again. Sitting in the tree next to my sister, our fingers peeling bark as we count the many different notes all made by the same bird, and know that every one has travelled thousands and thousands of miles.

But then I open my eyes. Because even though it sounds like home, it doesn't feel like it. Because she isn't here to hear it with me.

Nightingale chicks spend only ten to twelve days in the nest

The nightingale sings. Just like Rosie said when we were in the tree together the other week. It's here and she found it.

'Rosie?' I shout.

The nightingale sings.

'Rosie?' I shout again.

The nightingale sings back.

I look around and around. For her purple car parked up in the bays. For her eyes peering out of the bushes, bright with lights. For her finger on her lips telling me to stop being so stupid and shut up and listen to the everything with her.

I breathe and breathe. But the air isn't getting into my lungs and I'm just floating into nothing, up up up.

I shake my head and stumble forwards, tripping up on fallen twigs. Bouncing off one branch and then another, I search frantically through the trees.

'Rosie!' I shout louder.

The shadows are reaching into my chest now and curling their fingers in between my ribs, and it feels worse than any stitch I ever got in football or any time I was almost caught on this entire journey.

'You promised. You promised,' I say, spinning. 'I walked all this way and I was supposed to find you, like I found Buster and the leg tag and the football. And I did everything I could, Rosie, I really did. So stop hiding!'

The echo of my own voice comes back at me from the trees like I'm the one who's lost.

I don't have my mountain whistle or stepping stones to hop over. I can't see Rosie when I crouch down low and look under things, or even when I try to climb one of the trees to find her at the top.

I run, stumble and run some more, touching trees and looking up and down and around and screaming Rosie's name over and over, but nothing makes her appear. I've dropped my map somewhere, so now I'm lost along with her and I wonder if she sees all this darkness where she is, too.

'Please,' I say, but I'm just whispering now. 'This is the Better Place. Being with me is the Better Place.'

My knees hit the ground and it feels spongy and wet, but that is better than feeling all of this badness. So I push my hands into the grass and clutch it, tight.

I listen to the nightingale sing. But no one is singing back.

BIRD FACT #32

Caged nightingales often die in their desperation to migrate

Someone is calling my name.

'Jasper!'

They sound far away, but maybe that's because one of my ears is in the mud.

'Rosie?' I say, lifting my head up.

'Jasper!'

'Rosie!'

I stagger up and follow the sound, wrapped up in nightingale song. Out through the trees I see the light of the service station flashing blue and—

I stop and grip the tree to keep me from falling again.

'Jasper! Where are you?'

The person calling me isn't Rosie. I can hear that now I can see it.

It's Mum.

She's hugging herself around the middle and her cardigan is done up wrong. Dad is over to the side with some police officers, who have these blue lights that are flashing up into the trees. And the worry on both of their faces looks real – just like the news article said.

But that means the news article said something else true. And that is circling under me like a shark with big teeth waiting to bite and I'm scared.

I hug myself around a tree. I put my head up to it like I can make myself turn into wood that doesn't have to hear that something *tragic* has happened.

'Jasper?!' Mum says, and I know she has seen me,

but I don't want to look at her. 'Carl! Carl, he's here, Jasper is here!'

They both come running, along with the police officers in their big black boots. And Mum is crying and I don't think I've ever seen her cry and it's scary. And Dad's voice sounds broken too.

'Jasper,' Mum says, and her voice has big cracks in it that I think I might fall into. She reaches out her hands and it's too much and so I let go of the tree and step back.

She stops. So does Dad.

We just look at each other and there are all these words we aren't saying just flying around between us and *still* the nightingale sings.

I open my mouth. And I wonder if my own words can stop a bird from singing for ever.

'Where's the Better Place?'

Mum grabs hold of Dad like she might fall over, but he's looking wobbly himself.

'Where's Rosie?!' I say, much louder.

And they don't need to reply, because it is all over them written in big letters.

'Jasper, we thought you understood,' Dad says. 'We thought . . .' He swallows. And then he crouches down, grabs my hand and says it. Properly this time. 'Jasper, I'm so sorry. Rosie died last week. She passed away. She's gone.'

His voice breaks.

And I wonder for a moment what he's sorry for? That he missed all my birthdays because he was working. That he didn't listen to me.

Or that my sister Rosie is dead.

The shark under me leaps up to take a huge bite and I do the only thing I could ever possibly do when faced with that many teeth.

Run.

The average lifespan of a nightingale is two years

All the trees are monsters.

It used to be that they were homes for me and birds, but now I see that their branches have claws. They reach for me and rip as I run past, trying to trip me up from under the ground with their roots.

The police are following me, but they don't know

where I'm going because neither do I. I just need to get away from those words and I must be winning, because the trees start to disappear and there's a fence that I smash into so hard, I bounce back.

On the other side of the fence is the motorway, its cars roaring louder than lions, each one telling me that I can't walk through them.

But I can do anything. I walked all the way here.

I step my foot onto the bottom of the fence and start to climb.

'Your nightingale is very loud.'

The voice comes from next to me and I spin round, nearly dropping to the floor. It's Ibrahim. Leaning against the fence like he's been waiting for me.

I swallow. 'They're one of the loudest birds,' I say with a wobble in my voice. 'They can get even louder if there's noise around trying to out-sing them, like a motorway. I read they can be as loud as a chainsaw.'

Ibrahim comes closer to me and rests his arms on the top of the fence, looking at the swarm of cars over the other side. 'It's a very beautiful song,' he says. 'I can see now why you walked all this way.'

I can feel tears coming at the back of my eyes

like needles. 'I walked here for her. To find her. But she's not . . .'

It's dark here in the trees.

'Not all lost things are found in the same way, you know,' he says. 'Heart endures where eye doesn't see,' and he puts his hand over his heart, which doesn't make sense, because you can't see or hear or feel or taste anything with that.

I wipe my eyes with the back of my hand. 'What is it, Ibrahim? The piece of paper in your pocket.'

He freezes for a moment, but then takes it out slowly, looking at it for a moment all to himself before turning it around so I can see as best I can in the almost dark.

It's a photograph. I know it's old, because it's in black and white. But on it is a man wearing a white shirt, who I think is Ibrahim when he was probably the same age as my dad. He's standing next to a woman with long, dark hair and a big smile. And they're both holding guitars and looking like the whole world is their own.

'My wife,' he says, tracing his finger over her face. 'Leyla. Her soul bird flew away seven years ago.'

I remember that he called the bee a soul bird when it died on my finger.

'I'm sorry, Ibrahim,' I say, and I am. I feel like

my bones are filled with sorry and like my ribs are breaking with the weight of it. I grip the fence, tight. 'Rosie. Her soul bird . . .'

Ibrahim nods. 'Soul birds fly away. But the people we love stay with us always.'

He taps his chest again and I don't know whether he is touching his heart, or the picture of his wife, or whether they're the same thing, but I cling to the wood of the fence with all the strength I have left.

The nightingale is still singing and I want it to stop now, because it's strange that something so good can be going on when all this bad is happening.

'I'm sorry I couldn't help you find your lost thing, Ibrahim,' I whisper.

He squeezes my shoulder. 'Oh, but you did, Jasper.'

I want to say that I didn't help him at all and that I'm sorry for being mean, but my throat is clogged up. He keeps his hand on my shoulder anyway and it feels like maybe he's keeping me up on my feet. I suppose that's what friends do.

He hands me back my backpack. 'We should go and see your parents now. They're worried about you.'

I feel the outline of the *Book of Birds* in my bag and I nod.

It's good to have Ibrahim walking back next to me. Because there are some things that maybe you can't do alone, even when you're as used to looking after yourself as I am.

BIRD FACT #34

Nightingales are thought to be symbols of love

There is a whole crowd of police waiting for us and an ambulance too. I think the police are going to arrest me for causing all this fuss, but they don't. They just check that I'm okay and ask a lot of questions to Ibrahim, and then use their radio to stop the search for Jasper Wilde. The ambulance people check me over, but other than my sore feet and insides, I'm fine.

One of the officers gets in the car with Mum and Dad. I don't want to go with them, but I do because I'm so tired.

I don't want Mum to sit with me in the back and hold my hand so tight, but I let her because she looks afraid, Dad too. His eyes are wide and white in the mirror as he drives. I don't think he's watching the road much.

It doesn't even take us an hour to get home. I look out of the window and try to remember the places I've walked, but it looks different in the dark. All I see is a pheasant in the hedge, looking out at me as if he's wondering if I'm okay.

I don't think I am okay, because I walked a long way to find my sister and she wasn't there. And now she's dead and that means that she won't ever be there again, and that's the worst thought I've ever had. I should be panicking, because I worry over things a million times smaller than this all the time, but the sadness has pushed my panic away for now. I just sit with my head on the window, looking at the lights blurring by and the shadows sweeping in.

When we get into the house, Dad and the police officer want to sit down and have a conversation, but I don't want to talk to them. So I go upstairs and into my room. And Fish the cat tries to follow me, but I close the door, so she can't get in.

And I don't brush my teeth or put on my pyjamas or even read anything in the *Book of Birds*. I just climb into bed and sleep.

No bird on earth is completely silent

I wake up, forgetting everything, and the sun is out and shining on my pillow. My first thought is that maybe Rosie is coming to visit today, but then I remember that she can't and it feels like being stabbed in the belly.

I want to call Rosie and ask her to draw a swallow on my hand again and make the sadness go away, but when I do, all I get is her answering machine again and again. It feels like I'm standing on the edge of a cliff that's crumbling away and once I fall, there'll be a big black sea waiting to take me.

When I go downstairs, Mum is staring into space and Dad is holding on to her tight, but they both stop doing that when they see me and make a place for me between them on the sofa. I don't go to sit in it though. I stand at the door and hold on to the frame.

'Why didn't you listen to me?' I ask.

Mum fiddles with the buttons on her cardigan and it's annoying and I wish she would stop. 'I know, Jasper. We should have been there for you more – we know this now and we're so sorry, sweetheart. Your dad and I were so upset too, and I suppose we thought that by distracting ourselves with funeral preparations, we could—'

'You told me that she was in a Better Place. You told me that, but now she's gone away for ever instead and I wish it was you. I wish it was you and not her!'

I'm shouting now and I don't know why, but I'm angry like my skin is on fire and I want to smash a lot of things, but I don't seem to be moving. I'm just holding on to the door frame and shaking like an earthquake. But Mum looks like I really have smashed things into her, as her face is crumbling.

'Rosie was right. Rosie always said you were never here and you never listened and she was right. You didn't. And it's all your fault!'

Dad stands up and walks quickly towards me, and I think he is going to close the door on me, but he doesn't.

He holds me. Tight.

I kick and thrash and shout and thump his back with my fists and say *no no no no no*, but he holds me, and he doesn't stop to go to work, and his body feels like it's strong enough to stop mountains falling down.

'That's enough, Jasper.'

I stop trying to hurt him and let him carry me to the sofa.

'We were so worried about you,' he says. 'We thought we'd explained properly what happened, but we didn't. We just didn't want to hurt you, kiddo. And those words . . . they're hard for us to say, too. Now we see that maybe not saying them ended up hurting you more, and we're so sorry. We should have just told you the truth.'

He's still holding me tight.

'When we saw your note, we called everyone we knew and the police put out a missing child notice. So many people called in to say they'd seen you – on a bus, in a cow field, and even in a garden shed! But we didn't know what to believe, because it's such a long way to walk on your own, Jasper. Such a long way.'

I want to tell them that I got there. On my own without them. But that's not what I say.

'How did it happen?'

Dad doesn't speak for a moment and I think I can hear his own cliff falling away under his feet, and even though I'm still mad at him, I'm pleased that he's got me.

'It was – it was a car crash, Jasper. I'm sorry.'

And then he tells me the truth. He tells me that my Rosie died in her car, with the feather seats and the sunshine music. On her way home to pick me up, so we could find the nightingale together, just as she promised. There was an accident and she died, just like that.

I'd thought maybe she had died jumping into a reservoir to save a kitten again. Or climbing onto the roof of a house because she does it all the time. An accident isn't how Rosie should die. She wanted to save the world, and instead the world just took her. And it's not fair.

So I shout it at Mum and Dad who just keep hugging me. They don't tell me that everything is okay, because it isn't.

I'm in a cold black sea. But instead of drowning –
there are hands. Two hands. Holding mine and pulling
me up to where the air is.

And I try to remember to breathe.

BIRD FACT #36

Long-tailed tits couldn't build their nests without the help of spiders

There are a lot of people who want to talk to me from school and newspapers, but I don't really want to speak to any of them.

The same police officer who rode with us in the car

comes back on Tuesday morning though and asks me for a conversation just with her alone, at the kitchen table.

She's not wearing a uniform like the police officers at the supermarket were. Instead, she's wearing a blouse with a feather pattern on it and her hair is tied into a neat nest on the top of her head. Her name is Avery, and she lets me speak to her for a long time about aviaries, which are a type of home for birds at the zoo. She lets me tell her a lot of facts about them and other birds, before she asks me about my walk.

I feel stupid telling her that I thought Rosie would be waiting for me with the nightingale, because I know now that would have been impossible. I think I even knew that all along. But Avery tells me that sometimes when a bad thing happens, it can take a while to come to terms with it. I just wanted Rosie to be okay so much, I thought I could turn it into a fact.

I thought Avery might shout at me for walking all that way on my own, but she doesn't. She's pleased to hear about all the things I did to keep myself safe when I went, like not crossing roads without looking and taking the right food and water. She's less pleased to hear about me talking to strangers and tells me that next time I want to go on a walk, I should tell a grown-up in person and then take someone responsible with me who I know, because it could have been very dangerous.

I promise her that I will. And I say sorry again for making everyone panic and that it's not what I meant at all.

She looks at me with eyes that are pine-tree green. 'It's not your fault, Jasper. None of this is your fault. Please remember that – it's very important.'

It's just like Ibrahim said. The bravest thing anyone can do is tell their truth. And I'm going to do my best to be brave enough to keep telling mine.

After my talk with Avery, I go outside and find Dad in Rosie's wildlife hide, with his head in his hands.

I wanted to see the nails that Rosie had hammered into the wood at wonky angles, but the silence inside the hide is thick like caramel with Dad in there.

I go to sneak away, but he hears me.

'Jasper?' he says, looking up. 'Sit down.'

He shuffles across the bench even though there's plenty of room already. I keep standing at the door for a moment, wondering if I should run away from Dad's grey face and tired eyes.

'Please,' he says.

I inch in and sit down, slowly.

The hide smells hot from the sun and we can hear flies buzzing in the corners. But outside, the garden is green, fresh and alive. The bird seed that Rosie hooked up to a feeder in the middle of the overgrown lawn is spinning slowly in the breeze and we watch as a robin flutters down to a nearby perch, checks the coast is clear and then flies up to steal his dinner.

'Tell me about the birds,' Dad says, in a quiet voice.

I look at him. 'You never wanted to hear about birds before. You never listened.'

He opens his mouth and then closes it again. 'Did you know that it was Rosie who came up with the idea that we make the nut bars into a business?'

I shake my head.

'It was,' he says. 'I thought it would be nice – a way to bring us all together as a family. But then she stopped caring about making bars with her old dad, and became all about wildlife. And it was foxes this, and birds that. Twenty-four-seven, day and night. And then she started on it with you, and suddenly you were just the same.

And I—' He rubs his face. 'You're right, Jasper. I should have stopped trying to make her listen to me. I should have listened to her instead. And to you.'

He stops talking and the sticky silence comes back in, making the thick air difficult to breathe. I poke at my finger, where the bee stung me. You can't even see it now, even though it hurt when it happened, and I wonder if that's the same with everything that hurts. Panic starts to flutter in my chest and I take big, deep breaths to stop it building. But I forget to count them properly, so I just make it worse.

Dad stretches out his hand and takes mine, tight.

'The birds, Jasper. Tell me about them.'

'Robins.' I gasp. 'Robins can sing at night next to street lights. Their songs are different at different times of the year. They're one of the first birds to sing in the morning and one of the last to stop in the evening.'

My breathing starts going back to normal as I talk, until I feel okay again. And I stand up to go and leave Dad alone again, but he keeps hold of my hand.

'Stay,' he says, his eyes on the birds now flocking all at once to the bird feeder. 'I'm listening.'

Many birds don't return to the same nest again, once they've left it

I haven't read the *Book of Birds* since everything happened. But now it's Thursday and Mum said it's time for me to think about going back to school tomorrow, and I'm panicking.

The book used to stop me from worrying that much, but it feels like I'm panicking all the time at the moment and I thought that reading about Rosie might make it worse.

But I just found the coins in my pocket that I was saving to buy us chips, and it's made me miss her so much that I think I might explode. So, I climb into bed and sit with my knees up and the book on my lap. Taking a deep breath, I open the very front page and start reading.

I read about the different birds and how Rosie helped me find them. I read about the things she taught me to do and the things she did that she probably shouldn't have. I read it and it's like she's reading with me, because it's our book together and it's alive when she isn't.

When I get to the end there are still lots of blank pages at the back, waiting for us to fill them up with more adventures. But there won't be any more, because now she's gone and the story is over.

The last story in there is the one where Rosie found the dead crow on the side of the road, and I don't think that's the right ending at all. And then there are the words that Rosie wrote herself, expecting a story, but only getting an ending.

Rosie and Jasper's hunt
for the nightingale
NEXT WEEKEND

I can't write any of the things from my walk in it, because this is our book together – not mine without her. Even though I found the nightingale and she helped even though she wasn't there, it doesn't feel right.

So I take the coins from my pocket and they're like five little full stops. I stick them in the book, together in a circle with Sellotape. And I think for a long time what to write, but nothing seems like the right words, so I just draw a swallow like the one she drew on my hand, and hope that one day, we'll find each other again, and I can keep my promise to buy her some chips.

BIRD FACT #38

It's not too late to help save the nightingale

A whole lot of things can happen in a year. Like I can turn ten, even though Rosie stayed the same age, which is strange. And I can start writing a whole new book, because I couldn't fill up those blank pages in our *Book of Birds* all by myself. I hope she's reading the new one though. It feels good to talk to her again.

Years can be bad and good, but mostly they have a bit of both mixed up in them, and that's what this past year without Rosie has been like.

Going back to school was difficult at first, because everyone knew about Rosie and my walk. Ms Li was really nice though, and there were lots of other teachers there I could talk to or even sit in silence with when I needed to. The best part was when Gan moved house last June and suddenly appeared in my classroom as the new boy starting at my school.

As soon as we saw each other, we ran and gave each other a huge hug, with everyone in the class looking at us and wondering what was going on. Gan was saying sorry a lot, because he did tell his mum that I'd been in the garden. He said he was worried about me and only wanted to help. I told him that it was the right thing to do, and that he was also right when he said that sometimes it's better to know the truth about something, even when that thing is a broken football, or a sister who died in a car accident.

Gan sat next to me in class and helped me when I panicked or felt especially sad, which happened sometimes out of nowhere. It happened sometimes to Gan, too, so it felt nice to be able to look out for him in the same way. We played football with the other kids in my class and it turns out that most of them are good at helping too – if I just let them. We have lots of friends now, but Gan is still my best friend. It feels like maybe hidden under our skin, we share the same feathers.

Next year, Gan and I will be moving up to secondary school, and even though that's scary for both of us, we also know we have Lulu there to look out for us. We sometimes see her when we're walking home from school and she'll walk with us, telling us all about Buster's latest escape attempts.

Lulu and her grandma also managed to track down Madge, who invited me and Mum and Dad to have tea with her at her farm. She introduced me to her new budgies, who she named Jack and Jasper after the jackdaw and me. Jasper the budgie is yellow-green and sat on my shoulder like I was a pirate. And I turned round to laugh about that with Rosie, and then remembered suddenly that she wasn't there. But Mum was. And even though I was upset, Mum made pirate noises and pretended to blast me with cannons until I laughed again.

The other good thing that happened is Mel. Mel is Rosie's age, but she's different. She rides a bicycle and has a ring through her nose and doesn't even like wildlife. Rosie probably wouldn't have liked her very much, to be honest, but I do. Anyway, Mel is the new seedy-nut bar assistant, and she comes to the study every day to work with Mum and Dad when I'm at school. But then they lock the door to the study when she's gone and give me the key. This whole year they've been taking me to places on time and making me dinners. And I kept expecting them to let me down, but they haven't. Not once.

And then there's Ibrahim. He's been over to the house for dinner a lot and even got his face on the new seedy-nut bar. It turns out that Mum, Dad and Ibrahim have all these things in common, like music and recipes, and Ibrahim has probably become their friend too now. He even talked Dad into joining the Dunton Mayfield Junior Ramblers, so now they walk together at the back, making sure no one is left behind.

Sometimes I walk with the Junior Ramblers too, but mainly I just walk with Ibrahim. He taught me that having two pairs of socks on can help, because you get fewer blisters that way, and I taught him a lot about birds. We listen to them and he sings to them and they sing back. When I'm walking with Ibrahim, it feels like

I'm leaving the sadness behind for a bit and I'm free, like taking off a heavy bag every once in a while.

It's May again now, which means we've had new school terms and Christmas and birthdays without Rosie. But I've been afraid of this time more than all the others put together.

It's time to listen to the nightingale.

Mum and Dad have a plan though, and they've invited my granny over and Ibrahim too – because he's family now – to have a memorial for Rosie in the field behind our house.

Mum holds my hand and we all go through the back door together – fussing over turning the lights off, and carrying camping chairs. We walk in a line with Fish the cat at the front and Ibrahim laughing gently as he helps my granny at the back, all the way to the end of the garden and into the field towards the big tree.

And the light is leaking from the sky like someone has pulled a plug, and all the other birds are singing their lullabies. It smells like it's been raining, and water is still clinging to the grass and bushes.

We all sit together in a circle, snuggled under blankets, and Fish stretches and falls asleep on Granny's lap. Dad makes a speech that isn't very good because he keeps crying, but I think everyone understands it anyway. He tells the story about when Rosie knew about the bull in the field. He also talks about her saving Fish the cat from the reservoir, who starts purring at the mention of her name. Dad says that he's still a bit mad about that one, but leans over to give her chin a tickle.

Mum and Granny speak together, remembering when Rosie wore the same badger jumper to school for a week and how she was always diving into trouble when she was a baby. They talk about how they miss her and about how it isn't fair that she's gone. But also about how she'll be with them always in their hearts.

Ibrahim taps his heart pocket twice, too, and nods to me.

And then it's my turn to talk. Mum asked me before and I said that I wanted to say something. But then I kept trying to write things down and it all sounded wrong.

So Ibrahim and I came up with a new idea.

Mum gives me a kiss and Dad squeezes my leg and they bend over and whisper:

'You don't need to do this if it's too much.'

But I keep thinking how Rosie would want me to be brave. So I stand up, and lick my lips because they're feeling dry. And I say:

'I wanted to say beautiful things about my sister Rosie, because she was my everything. But humans aren't always the best at beautiful things, so I'm hoping our everything will say it instead.'

I look up to the tree, because the sun is all-the-way down now and it's time.

Mum kisses my head and tells me to be careful. And I nod and start climbing to the place where it all began.

The tree feels the same in my hands as always, but it isn't. Nothing is. Not even me. I still want to run away and hide from that, but there aren't enough map squares to keep some things the same.

I get to the flat branch and hold on, tight. And my family below stop talking and fall silent.

We listen.

We hear the long-off sounds of the main road and someone laughing. We hear each other breathing and our hands rubbing together. And we listen and we listen for the nightingale.

And slowly, it gets darker and darker.

I feel my stomach aching again, because I know then

that it isn't coming. The nightingale. And I know that nightingale numbers are going down and down, and I know that someone came and cut the bushes down in the field which is their home, but I hoped that it would be back at least for this year. Just so I can hear it one last time.

Just so it can help me say goodbye.

Then something soft and low comes from below. My heart backflips because I think for a moment that it's the nightingale, but it isn't. It's Ibrahim, singing. But his song has journeys inside it that could stretch as far as Africa and back if it wanted to.

I think about a lot of things as I listen to Ibrahim's song: how the nightingale didn't turn up today, but that the bushes are growing again, slowly, so maybe it will come back next year or the one after that. And I think about how I didn't find Rosie, even though I walked a long way and did everything I could.

But also, listening to Ibrahim sing, I realize that I probably did find quite a lot else. Like a mum and dad who keep their promises to be there. And friends who make me feel less alone. And I think about how some of the things you find, you get to carry with you for ever.

I hear Rosie whisper in the notes. 'It was brave of

you to climb this tree again, Jasper.'

And I whisper back. 'I know.'

And she says. 'Are you going to be okay?'

And I shake my head, because I'm not okay and being in our tree without her feels strange. But then I nod because I can see people below me who would be there to catch me if I fell. Mum. Dad. Granny. Ibrahim. And all the other people I met on my hunt for the nightingale out there somewhere, too.

Ibrahim lifts his head and sings into the stars.

I close my eyes. I take a deep breath.

And I listen.

AUTHOR'S NOTE

A few years ago, I was watching *Springwatch* in a hotel room when they covered an unusual sighting of a nightingale at a motorway service station. At that time, I'd never heard a nightingale sing before. I didn't really know anything about birds at all. But there was something about finding such a beautiful thing in such an unlikely place that had me packing my bag and setting off into the wilderness.

On my adventures, I discovered secret walking routes near to my house that I never knew existed. Although I mainly walked on my own, I met some amazing people along the way in cow fields, rivers and even waiting for the bus. I saw rainbow pheasants burst from bushes, murmurations of starlings that ribboned across sunset skies, and even walked through the night on a 100km Trailwalker trek for Oxfam.

Writing this book has taught me to listen – not only to the tapestry of birdsong you can often hear wherever you walk in the world, but also to other people. Volunteering for the NSPCC and working in schools, I met some brave and wonderful children who – just like Jasper – sometimes struggle with worries, anxiety and grief. The most important thing we can all do whenever we're feeling worried or upset is speak up to a trusted adult. And if someone chooses to trust us to talk to – we can listen.

If you or a child you know are experiencing some of Jasper's worries, there is plenty of help available. Ask a teacher or a responsible adult for help, or if you are an adult yourself, advice on grief can be found via Child Bereavement UK, or anxiety through Young Minds.

I did eventually hear a real nightingale sing; a lucky and wonderful thing, as nightingale numbers continue to drop as habitats change. In the dark and surrounded by other people on their own hunts, we listened to an orchestra of six nightingales from the shadows. And it felt more important than ever to protect this tiny bird that – despite being only slightly larger than a robin – can sing a breadth of notes like no other.

This book has inspired in me a lifelong love of birds and nature, as well as a sense of privilege that such wonderful things can be found right on our doorstep.

Thank you for sharing Jasper's journey with me and I hope the nightingale also inspires you to hunt for those everyday amazing things we can often find, if only we listen.

Sarah

ACKNOWLEDGEMENTS

There are so many people to thank for this book, but top of the list is my brilliant editor, Lucy Pearse. Lucy – your unwavering belief in this book continues to astound me, thank you so much. Thanks too to the entire S&S Children's team for their support.

I can't express just how much I love Sharon King-Chai's illustrations – thank you, Sharon, for agreeing to the incredibly tight deadlines and for bringing this story to life with such beauty. I am your biggest fan.

Thanks as always to Sallyanne Sweeney, who has actual magical powers. Thank you for continuing to choose to wield them for me.

To the many people who gave me editorial feedback on this book – thank you. Namely Rachael Cooper (who read it twice); Mum (who read it a billion times); Annie Rose; Anna Burtt; Pippa Lewis; Ellie Brough; Yasmin Rahman; Katya Balan; and the rest of you. Thanks also to my brilliant fact-checkers Pete Hughes and Demet Hoffmeyer-Zlotnik. And thank you to The Nest Collective and particularly Sam Lee for a truly magical night with the nightingale. With thanks to the Society of Authors and the Author's Foundation Grant, whose help made this book possible.

This book was inspired by so many people and it's impossible to list them all here. But I'd like to say a special thank you to *Springwatch*; Chris Packham; Oxfam Trailwalker; Farmer Deon and his cows; the writers at Retreats For You; and my team at Jericho Writers, past and present.

Writer-support thanks as always to Anna Raby, Harriet Venn and Kathryn Awde; my Brighton Ladies; and my work colleagues from all my many different jobs. Special shout-out to my wonderful author pals not already listed – you know who you are. Our MG vs YA escape room teams might need rethinking . . .

And lastly, a special thank you to my brilliant family. Mum and Dad, for everything you do. Louise, Jay, Amelia and Edward (to whom this book is dedicated). My wonderful grandparents. And Ryan Annis and family.

A good companion shortens the longest road – and how *lucky* I am to have all of you walking alongside me.

ABOUT THE AUTHOR

Sarah Ann Juckes writes books for young people. Her YA debut *Outside* (Penguin) was nominated for the Carnegie Medal Award 2020, shortlisted for Mslexia's Children's Novel Award, and longlisted for the Bath Children's Novel Award 2017. Her second YA novel, *The World Between Us* was published in March 2021, and *The Hunt for the Nightingale* is her first Middle Grade novel. She works with writers from all over the world via Jericho Writers and is on the board for Creative Future – a charity supporting under-represented writers. You can often find her hibernating in her writing shed in East Sussex, with her cat.

ABOUT THE ILLUSTRATOR

Sharon King-Chai is an award-winning designer and illustrator. Born in Australia, she moved to London in 2003 after completing an Honours degree in Visual Communication at the University of Technology Sydney, and has been based in north London ever since. Sharon has worked on a wide range of projects including album artwork, branding and logos, product packaging, book covers and event identities. Recent work includes collaborations with Julia Donaldson on the stunning and award-winning *Animalphabet* and *Counting Creatures*, as well as her solo picture book *Starbird*, winner of the Kate Greenaway Shadowers' Choice award 2021.